# A REIGN OF STEEL

### (BOOK #11 IN THE SORCERER'S RING)

## MORGAN RICE

"There is a land where food once grew—but its place was transformed, resembling fire. It was a place where stones were sapphires, and it had dust of gold."

"The horse laughs at fear, afraid of nothing; he does not shy from the sword. He cannot stand still when the trumpet sounds. At the blast of the trumpet, he snorts: 'Hurrah!'"

*--The Book of Job*

# CHAPTER ONE

Reece stood, the dagger in his hand impaled in Tirus's chest, frozen in a moment of shock. His entire world spun in slow motion, all of life a blur. He had just killed his worst enemy, the man responsible for Selese's death. For that, Reece felt a tremendous feeling of satisfaction, of vengeance. Finally, a great wrong had been set right.

Yet at the same time, Reece felt numb to the world, felt the odd feeling of preparing to greet death, bracing himself for the demise that would surely follow. The room was filled with Tirus's men, all of whom stood there, also frozen in shock, all witnessing the event. Reece braced himself for death. Yet he had no regrets. He felt grateful that he had even been given a chance to kill this man, who dared to think that Reece would ever actually apologize to him.

Reece knew that death was inevitable; he was too outnumbered in this room, and the only people in this great hall that were on his side were Matus and Srog. Srog, wounded, was bound with ropes, captive, and Matus stood beside him, under the watchful eye of the soldiers. They would be of little help against this army of Upper Islanders loyal to Tirus.

But before Reece died, he wanted to complete his revenge, and to take out as many of these Upper Islanders as he could.

Tirus slumped down to Reece's feet, dead, and Reece did not hesitate: he extracted his dagger and immediately spun and sliced the throat of Tirus's general, standing beside him; in the same motion, Reece whipped around and stabbed another general in the heart.

As the shocked room began to react, Reece moved quickly. He drew both swords from the scabbards of the two dying men, and charged the group of soldiers facing him. He killed four of them before they had a chance to react.

Hundreds of warriors finally broke into action, descending on Reece from all sides. Reece summoned all his training in the Legion, all the times he been forced to fight against groups of men, and as

7

they encircled him, he raised his sword with both hands. He wasn't weighed down by armor, like these other men, or by a belt full of weapons, or a shield; he was lighter and faster than them all, and he was enraged, cornered in, and fighting for his life.

Reece fought valiantly, faster than all of them, remembering all those times he had sparred against Thor, the greatest warrior he'd ever fought, remembering how much his skills had been sharpened. He took down man after man, his sword clanging against countless others, sparks flying as he fought in every direction. He swung and swung until his arms grew heavy, cutting down a dozen men before they could blink.

But more and more men poured in. There were just too many of them. For every six that fell, a dozen more appeared, and the crowd grew thick as they rallied and pressed on him from all sides. Reece was breathing hard as he felt a sword slash his arm, and he screamed out, blood coming from his bicep. He swung around and stabbed the man in the ribs, but the damage had already been done. He was wounded now, and still more men appeared from every side. He knew his time had come.

At least, he realized, grateful, he was able to go down in an act of valor.

"REECE!"

A shriek suddenly pierced the air, a voice that Reece recognized immediately.

A woman's voice.

Reece's body went numb as he realized whose voice it was. It was the voice of the one woman left in the world who could catch his attention, even in the midst of this great battle, even in the midst of his dying moments:

Stara.

Reece looked up and saw her standing high atop the wooden bleachers that lined the sides of the room. She stood high above the crowd, her expression fierce, veins bulging in her throat as she screamed for him. He saw she held a bow and arrow, and he watched as she took aim up high, at an object across the room.

Reece followed her gaze, and he realized what she aimed for: a thick rope, fifty feet long, anchoring an immense metal chandelier thirty feet in diameter, dropping to an iron hook in the stone floor. The fixture was as thick as a tree trunk, and held several hundred flaming candles.

Reece realized: Stara aimed to shoot out the cord. If she hit, it would send the chandelier crashing down—and it would crush half the men in this room. And as Reece looked up, he realized that he was standing right underneath it.

She was warning him to move.

Reece's heart pounded in panic as he turned and lowered his sword and charged wildly into his group of attackers, rushing to get out before it fell. He kicked and elbowed and head-butted soldiers out of his way as he burst through the group. Reece remembered from childhood what a great shot Stara was—always outdoing the boys—and he knew her aim would be true. Even though he ran with his back exposed to the men chasing him, he trusted her, knowing she would hit.

A moment later Reece heard the sound of an arrow slicing through the air, of a great rope snapping, then of a massive piece of iron releasing, plummeting straight down, rushing through the air at full speed. There came a tremendous crash, the entire room shaking, the vibration knocking Reece off his feet. Reece felt the wind on his back, the chandelier missing him by just a few feet as he fell to the stone on his hands and knees.

Reece heard the screams of men, and he looked over his shoulder and saw the damage Stara had done: dozens of men lay crushed beneath the chandelier, blood everywhere, crying out, pinned to their deaths. She had saved his life.

Reece scrambled to his feet, looking for Stara, and saw that she was in danger now. Several men were closing in on her, and while she took aim with her bow and arrow, he knew there were only so many shots she could get off.

She turned and looked nervously to the door, clearly thinking they could escape that way. But as Reece followed her glance, his heart dropped to see dozens of Tirus's men rush forward and block it, barring the two huge double doors with a thick wooden beam.

They were trapped, all exits blocked. Reece knew they would die here.

Reece saw Stara looking about the room, frantic, until her eyes settled on the uppermost row of the wooden bleachers along the back wall.

She gestured to Reece as she ran for it, and he had no idea what she had in mind. He saw no exit there. But she knew this castle better than he, and perhaps had an escape route in mind that he could not see.

Reece turned and ran, fighting his way through the men as they began to regroup and attack him. As he sprinted through the crowd, he fought minimally, trying not to engage them too much, but rather trying to cut a singular path through the men and make his way to the far corner of the room.

As he ran, Reece looked over at Srog and Matus, determined to help them, too, and he was happily surprised to see that Matus had grabbed the swords of his captors and had stabbed them both; he watched as Matus quickly cut Srog's cords, freeing Srog, who grabbed a sword and killed several soldiers who approached.

"Matus!" Reece screamed.

Matus turned and looked to him, and he saw Stara along the far wall and saw where Reece was running. Matus yanked Srog, and they turned and ran for it, too, all of them now heading in the same direction.

As Reece fought his way through the room, it began to open up. There were not as many soldiers here in this far corner of the room, far away from the opposite corner, from the barred exit where all the soldiers were converging. Reece hoped that Stara knew what she was doing.

Stara ran along the wooden bleachers, jumping higher and higher up the rows, kicking men in the face as they reached up to grab her. As Reece watched her, trying to catch up, he still did not know exactly where she was going, or what her plan could be.

Reece reached the far corner and jumped up onto the bleachers, jumping onto the first wooden row, then the next, then the next, climbing higher and higher, till he was a good ten feet above the crowd, on the farthest, highest wooden bench against the wall. He met up with Stara, and they converged against the far wall with Matus and Srog. They had a good lead on the other soldiers, except for one: he rushed Stara from behind, and Reece lunged forward and stabbed him through the heart, right before he brought a dagger down on Stara's back.

Stara raised her bow and turned to two soldiers lunging for Reece's exposed back, swords drawn, and took out them both.

The four of them stood, backs to the wall in the far corner of the room, on the highest bleacher, and Reece looked out and saw a hundred men race across the room, closing in on them. They were trapped now in this corner, with nowhere to go.

Reece did not understand why Stara had led them all here. Seeing no possible means of escape, he was certain that they would soon all be dead.

"What is your plan?" he yelled to her, as they stood side by side, fighting off men. "There is no way out!"

"Look up," she replied.

Reece craned his neck and saw above them another iron chandelier, with a long rope leading from it all the way down to the floor, right beside him.

Reece's brow furrowed in confusion.

"I don't understand," he said.

"The rope," she said. "Grab it. All of you. And hold on for dear life."

They did as she instructed, each grabbing the rope with both hands and holding tight. Suddenly, Reece realized what Stara was about to do.

"Are you sure this is a good idea?" he called out.

But it was too late.

As a dozen soldiers approached them, Stara grabbed Reece's sword, jumped into Reece's arms, and slashed the rope beside them, the one holding the chandelier.

Reece felt his stomach drop as suddenly the four of them, clutching onto the rope and each other, shot up high into the air at a dizzying speed, grabbing on for dear life as the iron chandelier plummeted down. It crushed the men below them and propelled the four of them high into the air, swinging from the rope.

The rope finally stopped, and the four of them hung there, swinging in the air, a good fifty feet above the hall.

Reece looked down, sweating, almost losing his grip.

"There!" Stara called out.

Reece turned and saw the huge stained-glass window before them, and realized her plan. The coarse rope cut Reece's palms, and he started to slip with the sweat. He didn't know how much longer he could hold on.

"I'm losing my grip!" Srog called out, trying his best to hold on despite his injuries.

"We need to swing!" Stara yelled. "We need momentum! Kick off the wall!"

Reece followed her lead: he leaned forward with his boot against the wall and together, they shoved off the wall, the rope swinging more and more wildly. They shoved again and again, until with one final kick, they swung all the way back, like a pendulum, and then they all, shouting, braced themselves as they swung right for the enormous stained-glass window.

The glass exploded, raining down all around them, and the four of them let go, dropping onto the wide stone platform at the base of the window.

Standing there, perched fifty feet above the room, the cold air rushing in, Reece looked down below, and on one side he saw the inside of the hall, hundreds of soldiers looking up at them, wondering how to pursue; on the other side he saw outside the fort. It was pouring outside, driving wind and blinding rain, and the drop below was a good thirty feet, certainly enough to break a leg. But Reece, at least, saw several tall bushes below, and he also saw that the ground was wet and soft with mud. It would be a long, hard fall; but maybe they would be cushioned enough.

Suddenly, Reece screamed out as he felt metal piercing his flesh. He looked down and grabbed his arm and realized an arrow had just grazed it, drawing blood. It was a minor wound, but it stung.

Reece turned and checked back down over his shoulder, and saw that dozens of Tirus's men were aiming bows and firing, arrows whizzing by them now from every direction.

Reece knew there was no time. He looked over and saw Stara standing on one side of him, Matus and Srog on the other, all of them wide-eyed with fear at the drop before them. He grabbed Stara's hand, knowing it was now or never.

Without a word, all of them knowing what needed to be done, they jumped together. They shrieked as they dropped through the air in the blinding rain and wind, flailing and falling, and Reece could not help but wonder if he'd just leapt from one certain death to another.

## CHAPTER TWO

Godfrey raised his bow with trembling hands, leaned over the edge of the parapet, and took aim. He meant to pick a target and fire right away—but as he saw the sight below, he knelt there, frozen in shock. Below him charged thousands of McCloud soldiers, a well-trained army flooding the landscape, all heading right for the gates of King's Court. Dozens of them rushed forward with an iron battering ram, and slammed it into the iron portcullis again and again, shaking the walls, the ground beneath Godfrey's feet.

Godfrey lost his balance and fired, and the arrow sailed harmlessly through the air. He grabbed another arrow and pulled it back on the bow, his heart pounding, knowing for sure that he would die here today. He leaned over the edge, but before he could fire, a rock cast from a sling flew up and smacked into his iron helmet.

There was a loud clang, and Godfrey fell back, his arrow shooting straight up into the air. He yanked off his helmet and rubbed his aching head. He never knew a rock could hurt so much; the iron seemed to reverberate in his very skull.

Godfrey wondered what he had gotten himself into. True, he had been heroic, he had helped by alerting the entire city of the McClouds' arrival, buying them precious time. He had maybe even saved some lives. He had certainly saved his sister.

Yet now here he was, along with but a few dozen soldiers left here, none of them Silver, none of them knights, defending this shell of an evacuated city against an entire McCloud army. This soldier stuff was not for him.

There came a tremendous crash, and Godfrey stumbled again as the portcullis was smashed open.

In through the open city gates rushed thousands of men, cheering, out for blood. As he sat up on the parapet, Godfrey knew it

14

was only a matter of time until they came up here, until he'd fight his way to the death. Was this what it meant to be a soldier? Was this what it meant to be brave and fearless? To die, so others could live? Now that he was greeting death in the face, he wasn't so sure this was a great idea. Being a soldier, being a hero, was great; but being alive was better.

As Godfrey thought of quitting, of running off and trying to hide somewhere, suddenly, several McClouds stormed the parapets, racing up single file. Godfrey watched as one of his fellow soldiers was stabbed and dropped to his knees, groaning.

And then, once again, it happened. Despite all his rational thinking, all his common wisdom against being a soldier, something clicked inside Godfrey that he could not control. Something inside Godfrey could not stand to let other people suffer. For himself, he could not muster the courage; but when he saw his fellow man in trouble, something overcame him—a certain recklessness. One might even call it chivalry.

Godfrey reacted without thinking. He found himself grabbing a long pike and charging for the row of McClouds who raced up the stairs, single file along the parapets. He let out a great scream and, holding the pike firm, he rammed the first man. The huge metal blade went into the man's chest, and Godfrey ran, using his weight, even his beer belly, to push them all back.

To his own amazement, Godfrey succeeded, driving the row of men back down the spiral stone staircase, back down away from the parapets, single-handedly holding off the McClouds storming the place.

When he finished, Godfrey dropped the pike, amazed at himself, not knowing what had come over him. His fellow soldiers looked amazed too, as if not realizing he had it in him.

As Godfrey wondered what to do next, his decision was made for him, as he detected motion from the corner of his eye. He turned and saw a dozen more McClouds charging him from the side, pouring into the other side of the parapets.

Before Godfrey could manage to put up a defense, the first soldier reached him, wielding a huge war hammer, swinging for his head. Godfrey realized that the blow would crush his skull.

Godfrey ducked out of harm's way—one of the few things he knew how to do well—and the hammer swung over his head. Godfrey then lowered his shoulder and charged the soldier, driving him backwards, tackling him.

Godfrey drove him back, further and further, to where they grappled along the edge of the parapet, fighting hand-to-hand, grabbing for each other's throats. This man was strong, but Godfrey was strong, too, one of the few gifts he had been graced with in his life.

The two clambered, spinning each other back and forth, until suddenly, they both rolled over the edge.

The two of them went plummeting through the air, clutching each other, falling a good fifteen feet down to the ground below. Godfrey spun in the air, hoping that he would land on top of this soldier, instead of the other way around. He knew that the weight of this man, and all his armor, would crush him.

Godfrey spun at the last second, landing on the man, and the soldier groaned as Godfrey's weight crushed him, knocking him out.

But the fall took its toll on Godfrey, too, winding him; he hit his head, and as he rolled off the man, every bone in his body aching, Godfrey lay there for one second before the world spun, and he, lying beside his foe, blacked out beside him. The last thing he saw as he looked up was an army of McClouds, streaming into King's Court and taking it for their own.

\*

Elden stood in the Legion training grounds, hands on his hips, Conven and O'Connor beside him, the three of them watching over the new recruits Thorgrin had left them with. Elden watched with an expert eye as the boys galloped back and forth across the field, trying to leap over ditches and launch spears through hanging targets. Some boys did not make the jump, collapsing with their horses into the pits; others did, but missed the targets.

Elden shook his head, trying to remember how he was when he first started his Legion training, and trying to take encouragement in the fact that in the last few days these boys had already shown signs of improvement. Yet these boys were still nowhere near the hardened warriors he needed them to be before he could accept them as recruits. He set the bar very high, especially as he had a great responsibility to make Thorgrin and all the others proud; Conven and O'Connor, too, would allow nothing less.

"Sire, there is news."

Elden looked over to see one of the recruits, Merek, the former thief, come running up to him, wide-eyed. Interrupted from his thoughts, Elden was agitated.

"Boy, I told you to never interrupt—"

"But sire, you don't understand! You must—"

"No, YOU don't understand," Elden countered. "When the recruits are training, you don't—"

"LOOK!" Merek shouted, grabbing him and pointing.

Elden, in a rage, was about to grab Merek and throw him, until he looked out at the horizon, and he froze. He could not fathom the sight before him. There, on the horizon, great clouds of black smoke rose into the air. All from the direction of King's Court.

Elden blinked, not understanding. Could King's Court be on fire? How?

Great shouts arose on the horizon, the shouts of an army—along with the sound of a crashing portcullis. Elden's heart sank; the gates to King's Court had been stormed. He knew that could only mean one thing—a professional army had invaded. Today, of all days, on Pilgrimage Day, King's Court was being overrun.

Conven and O'Connor burst into action, shouting out to the recruits to stop what they were doing, and rounding them up.

The recruits hurried over, and Elden stepped forward beside Conven and O'Connor, as they all quieted and stood at attention, awaiting orders.

17

"Men," Elden boomed. "King's Court has been attacked!"

There came a surprised and agitated murmur from the crowd of boys.

"You are not yet Legion, and you are certainly not Silver or hardened warriors that would be expected to go up against a professional army. Those men invading there are invading to kill, and if you go up against them, you may very well lose your lives. Conven, O'Connor, and I are duty bound to protect our city, and we must leave now for war. I do not expect any of you to join us; in fact, I would discourage it. Yet if any of you wish to, step forward now, knowing you may very well die on the field of battle today."

There came a few moments of silence, then suddenly, every single boy standing before them stepped forward, all brave, noble. Elden's heart swelled with pride at the sight.

"You have all become men today."

Elden mounted his horse and the others followed, all of them letting out a great cheer as they charged forward as one, as men, to risk their lives for their people.

\*

Elden, Conven, and O'Connor led the way, a hundred recruits behind them, all galloping, weapons drawn, as they raced toward King's Court. As they neared, Elden looked out and was shocked to see several thousand McCloud soldiers storming the gates, a well-coordinated army clearly taking advantage of Pilgrimage Day to ambush King's Court. They were outnumbered ten to one.

Conven smiled, riding out in front.

"Just the kind of odds I like!" he shouted, taking off with a great cry, charging out in front of everyone, wanting to be the first to advance. Conven raised his battle-ax high, and Elden watched with admiration and concern as Conven recklessly attacked the rear of the McCloud army by himself.

The McClouds had little time to react as Conven swung his ax down like a madman and took out two of them at a time. Charging into the thick of the soldiers, he then dove from his horse and went flying through the air, tackling three soldiers and bringing them tumbling off their horse to the ground.

Elden and the others were right behind him. They clashed with the rest of the McClouds, who were too slow to react, not expecting an attack on their flank. Elden wielded his sword with wrath and dexterity, showing the Legion recruits how it was done, using his great might to take down one after the other.

The battle became thick and hand-to-hand, as their small fighting force forced the McClouds to change direction and defend. All the Legion recruits joined the fray, riding fearlessly into battle and clashing with the McClouds. Elden noticed the boys fighting out of the corner of his eyes and he was proud to see none of them hesitating. They were all in battle, fighting like real men, outnumbered hundreds to one, and none of them caring. McClouds fell left and right, caught off guard.

But the momentum soon turned, as the bulk of the McCloud men reinforced, and the Legion encountered professional soldiers. Some of the Legion began to fall. Merek and Ario took blows from a sword, but remained on their horses, fighting back and knocking their opponents down. But then they were hit by swinging flails, and knocked off their horses. O'Connor, riding beside Merek, got off several shots with his bow, taking out soldiers all around them— before being struck in the side with a shield and knocked off his horse. Elden, completely surrounded, finally lost the element of surprise, and he took a mighty blow to his ribs from a hammer, and a sword slash on his forearm. He turned and knocked the men off their horses—yet as he did, four more men appeared. Conven, on the ground, fought desperately, swinging his ax wildly at horses and men who charged by—until finally he was hit from behind by a hammer and collapsed face-first in the mud.

Scores more McCloud reinforcements arrived, abandoning the gate to face them. Elden saw fewer of his own men, and he knew that soon they would all be wiped out. But he didn't care. King's Court was under attack, and he would give up his life to defend it, to defend these Legion boys whom he was so proud to fight with. Whether they were boys or men no longer mattered—they were shedding their blood beside him, and on this day, alive or dead, they were all brothers.

*

Kendrick galloped down the mountain of pilgrimage, leading a thousand Silver, all of them riding harder than they ever had, racing for the black smoke on the horizon. Kendrick chided himself as he rode, wishing he had left the gates more protected, never expecting such an attack on a day like this, and most of all, from the McClouds, whom he thought were pacified under Gwen's rule. He would make them all pay for invading his city, for taking advantage of this holy day.

All around him his brothers charged, one thousand strong, the entire wrath of the Silver, forgoing their sacred pilgrimage, determined to show the McClouds what the Silver could do, to make the McClouds pay once and for all. Kendrick vowed that by the time he was done, not one McCloud would be left alive. Their side of the Highlands would never rise again.

As Kendrick neared, he looked ahead and spotted Legion recruits fighting valiantly, saw Elden and O'Connor and Conven, all terribly outnumbered, and none backing down to the McClouds. His heart soared with pride. But they were all, he could see, about to be vanquished.

Kendrick cried out and kicked his horse even harder as he led his men and they all burst forward in one last charge. He picked up a long spear and as he got close enough, he hurled it; one of the McCloud generals turned just in time to see the spear sail through the air and pierce his chest, the throw strong enough to penetrate his armor.

The thousand knights behind Kendrick let out a great shout: the Silver had arrived.

The McClouds turned and saw them, and for the first time, they had real fear in their eyes. A thousand shining Silver knights, all of them riding in perfect unison, like a storm coming down the mountain, all with weapons drawn, all hardened killers, none with an ounce of hesitation in their eyes. The McClouds turned to face them, but with trepidation.

The Silver descended upon them, upon their home city, Kendrick leading the charge. He drew his ax and swung expertly, chopping several soldiers from their horses; he then drew a sword with his other hand, and riding into the thick of the crowd, stabbed several soldiers in all the vulnerable points of their armor.

The Silver bore right through the mass of soldiers like a wave of destruction, as they were so expert at doing, none of them at home until they were completely surrounded in the thick of battle. For a member of the Silver, that's what it meant to be at home. They slashed and stabbed all the McCloud soldiers around them, who were like amateurs compared to them, cries rising greater and greater as they felled McClouds in every direction

No one could stop the Silver, who were too fast and sleek and strong and expert in their technique, fighting as one unit, as they had been trained to do since they could walk. Their momentum and skill terrified the McClouds, who were like common soldiers next to these finely trained knights. Elden, Conven, O'Connor and the remaining Legion, rescued by the reinforcements, rose back to their feet, however wounded, and joined the fight, helping the Silver's momentum even further.

Within moments, hundreds of McClouds lay dead, and those that remained were overtaken by a great panic. One by one, they began to turn and flee, McClouds pouring out of the city gates, trying to get away from King's Court.

Kendrick was determined not to let them. He rode to the city gates, his men following, and made sure to block the path of all those retreating. It was a funnel effect, and McClouds were slaughtered as they reached the bottleneck of the city gates—the very same gates they had stormed but hours before.

As Kendrick wielded two swords, killing men left and right, he knew that soon, every McCloud would be dead, and King's Court would be theirs once again. As he risked his life for the sake of his soil, he knew that this was what it meant to be alive.

21

# CHAPTER THREE

Luanda's hands trembled as she walked, one step at a time, across the vast Canyon crossing. With each step, she felt her life coming to an end, felt herself leaving one world and about to enter another. But steps away from reaching the other side, she felt as if these were her last steps on earth.

Standing just feet away was Romulus, and behind him, his million Empire soldiers. Circling high overhead, with an unearthly screeching, flew dozens of dragons, the fiercest creatures Luanda had ever laid eyes upon, slamming their wings against the invisible wall that was the Shield. Luanda knew that, with just a few more steps, with her leaving the Ring, the Shield would come down for good.

Luanda looked out at the destiny that stood waiting before her, at the sure death that she faced at the hands of Romulus and his brutal men. But this time, she no longer cared. Everything that she loved had already been taken from her. Her husband, Bronson, the man she loved most in the world, had been killed—and it was all Gwendolyn's fault. She blamed Gwendolyn for everything. Now, finally, it was time for vengeance.

Luanda stopped a foot away from Romulus, the two of them locking eyes, staring at each other over the invisible line. He was a grotesque man, twice as wide as any man should ever be, pure muscle, so much muscle in his shoulders that his neck disappeared. His face was all jaw, with roving, large black eyes, like marbles, and his head was too big for his body. He stared at her like a dragon looking down at its prey, and she had no doubt that he would tear her to pieces.

They stared each other in the thick silence, and a cruel smile spread across his face, along with a look of surprise.

"I never thought to see you again," he said. His voice was deep and guttural, echoing in this awful place.

Luanda closed her eyes and tried to make Romulus disappear. Tried to make her life disappear.

But when she opened her eyes, he was still there.

"My sister has betrayed me," she answered softly. "And now it is time for me to betray her."

Luanda closed her eyes and took one final step, off the bridge, onto the far side of the Canyon.

As she did, there came a thunderous whooshing noise behind her; swirling mist shot up into the air from the bottom of the Canyon, like a great wave rising, and just as suddenly dropped back down again. There was a sound, as of the earth cracking, and Luanda knew with certainty that the Shield was down. That now, nothing remained between Romulus's army and the Ring. And that the Shield had been broken forever.

Romulus looked down at her, as Luanda bravely stood a foot away, facing him, unflinching, staring back defiantly. She felt fear but did not show it. She did not want to give Romulus the satisfaction. She wanted him to kill her when she was staring him in the face. At least that would give her something. She just wanted him to get it over with.

Instead, Romulus's smile broadened, and he continued to stare directly at her, rather than at the bridge, as she expected he would.

"You have what you want," she said, puzzled. "The Shield is down. The Ring is yours. Aren't you going to kill me now?"

He shook his head.

"You are not what I expected," he finally said, summing her up. "I might let you live. I might even take you as my wife."

Luanda gagged inside at the thought; this was not the reaction she'd wanted.

She leaned back and spit in his face, hoping that would get him to kill her.

Romulus reached up and wiped his face with the back of his hand, and Luanda braced herself for the blow to come, expecting him to punch her as before, to shatter her jaw—to do anything but be nice to her. Instead, he stepped forward, grabbed her by the back of her hair, pulled her to him, and kissed her hard.

She felt his lips, grotesque, chapped, all muscle, like a snake, as he pressed her to him, harder and harder, so hard she could barely breathe.

Finally, he pulled away—and as he did, he backhanded her, smacking her so hard her skin stung.

She looked up at him, horrified, filled with disgust, not understanding him.

"Chain her and keep her close to me," he commanded. He had barely finished uttering the words before his men stepped forward and bound her arms behind her back.

Romulus's eyes widened with delight as he stepped forward in front of his men, and, bracing himself, took the first step onto the bridge.

There was no Shield to stop him. He stood there safe and sound.

Romulus broke into a wide grin, then burst out laughing, holding his muscular arms out wide as he flung back his head. He roared with laughter, with triumph, the sound echoing throughout the Canyon.

"It is mine," he boomed. "All mine!"

His voice echoed, again and again.

"Men," he added. "Invade!"

His troops suddenly rushed past him, letting out a great cheer that was met, high above, by the host of dragons, who flapped their wings and flew, soaring above the Canyon. They entered the swirling mist, screeching, a great noise that rose to the very heavens, that let the world know that the Ring would never be the same again.

24

## CHAPTER FOUR

Alistair lay in Erec's arms on the bow of the huge ship, which rocked gently up and down as the huge ocean waves rolled past again and again. She looked up, mesmerized, at the million red stars blanketing the night sky, sparkling in the distance; warm ocean breezes rolled in, caressing her, lulling her to sleep. She felt content. Just being here, together with Erec, her whole world felt at peace; here, in this part of the world, on this vast ocean, it felt as if all the troubles in the world had disappeared. Endless obstacles had kept the two of them apart and now, finally, her dreams were coming true. They were together, and there was no one and nothing left to stand between them. They had already set sail, were already on their way to his islands, his homeland, and when they arrived, she would marry him. There was nothing she wanted more in the world.

Erec squeezed her tight, and she leaned in closer to him as the two of them leaned back, looking up at the universe, the gentle ocean mist washing over them. Her eyes grew heavy in the quiet ocean night.

As she looked out at the open sky, she thought of how huge the world was; she thought of her brother, Thorgrin, out there somewhere, and she wondered where he was right now. She knew he was on his way to see their mother. Would he find her? What would she be like? Did she even really exist?

A part of Alistair wanted to join him on the journey, to meet their mother, too; and another part of her missed the Ring already, and wanted to be back home on familiar ground. But the biggest part of her was excited; she was excited to start life again, together with Erec, in a new place, a new part of the world. She was excited to meet his people, to see what his homeland was like. Who lived in the Southern Isles? she wondered. What were his people like? Would his family take him in? Would they be happy to have her, or would they be threatened by her? Would they welcome the idea of their wedding? Or had they envisioned someone else, one of their own, for Erec?

25

Worst of all, what she dreaded most—what would they think of her once they found out about her powers? Once they found out that she was a Druid? Would they consider her a freak, an outsider, like everyone else?

"Tell me again of your people," Alistair said to Erec.

He looked at her, then looked backed out at the sky.

"What would you like to know?"

"Tell me about your family," she said.

Erec reflected in the silence for a long time. Finally, he spoke:

"My father, he is a great man. He's been king of our people ever since he was my age. His looming death will change our island forever."

"And have you any other family?"

Erec hesitated a long time, then finally nodded.

"Yes. I have a sister…and a brother." He hesitated. "My sister and I, we were very close growing up. But I must warn you, she's very territorial and too easily jealous. She's wary of outsiders, and does not like new people in our family. And my brother…" Erec trailed off.

Alistair prodded him.

"What is it?"

"A finer fighter you will never meet. But he is my younger brother, and he has always set himself in competition with me. I have always viewed him as a brother, and he has always viewed me as competition, as someone who stands in his way. I do not know why. It just is how it is. I wish we could be closer."

Alistair looked at him, surprised. She could not understand how anyone could look at Erec with anything but love.

"And is it still that way?" she asked.

Erec shrugged.

"I have not seen any of them since I was a child. It is my first return to my homeland; nearly thirty sun cycles have passed. I do not know what to expect. I am more a product of the Ring now. And yet if my father dies…I am the eldest. My people will look to me to rule."

Alistair paused, wondering, not wanting to pry.

"And will you?"

26

Erec shrugged.

"It is not something I seek. But if my father wishes…I cannot say no."

Alistair studied him.

"You love him very much."

Erec nodded, and she could see his eyes glistening in the starlight.

"I only pray our ship arrives in time before he dies."

Alistair considered his words.

"And what of your mother?" she asked. "Would she like me?"

Erec smiled wide.

"Like a daughter," he said. "For she will see how much I love you."

They kissed, and Alistair leaned back and looked at the sky, reaching over and grasping Erec's hand.

"Just remember this, my lady. I love you. You above all else. That is all that matters. My people shall give us the greatest wedding that the Southern Isles have ever seen; they will shower us with every festivity. And you will be loved and embraced by all of them."

Alistair studied the stars, holding Erec's hand tight, and she wondered. She had no doubt of his love for her, but she wondered about his people, people he himself barely knew. Would they embrace her as he thought they would? She was not so sure.

Suddenly, Alistair heard heavy footsteps. She looked over to see one of the ship's crew walk over to the edge of the railing, hoist a large dead fish over his head, and throw it overboard. There was a gentle splash below, and soon a bigger splash, as another fish leapt up and ate it.

There then followed an awful sound in the waters below, like a moaning or crying, followed by another splash.

Alistair looked over at the sailor, an unsavory character, unshaven, dressed in rags, with missing teeth, as he leaned over the edge, grinning like an oaf. He turned and looked right at her, his face evil, grotesque in the starlight. Alistair got a terrible feeling as he did.

"What did you throw overboard?" Erec asked.

"The guts of a simka fish," he replied.

"But why?"

"It's poison," he replied, grinning. "Any fish that eats it dies on the spot."

Alistair looked at him, horrified.

"But why would you want to kill the fish?"

The man smiled more broadly.

"I like to watch them die. I like to hear them scream, and I like to see them float, belly up. It's fun."

The man turned and walked slowly back to the rest of his crew, and as Alistair watched him go, she felt her skin crawl.

"What is it?" Erec asked her.

Alistair looked away and shook her head, trying to make her feeling go away. But it would not; it was an awful premonition, she was not sure of what.

"Nothing, my lord," she said.

She settled back into his arms, trying to tell herself that everything was all right. But she knew, deep down, that it was very far from all right.

*

Erec woke in the night, feeling the ship moving slowly up and down, and he knew immediately that something was wrong. It was the warrior within him, the part of him that had always warned him an instant before something bad happened. He'd always had the sense, ever since he was a boy.

He sat up quickly, alert, and looked all around. He turned and saw Alistair soundly asleep beside him. It was still dark, the boat still rocking on the waves, yet something was wrong. He looked all around, but saw no sign of anything amiss.

What danger could there be, he wondered, out here in the middle of nowhere? Was it just a dream?

Erec, trusting his instincts, reached down to grab his sword. But before his hand could grab the hilt, he suddenly felt a heavy net covering his body, draping down all around him. It was made of the heaviest rope he'd ever felt, nearly heavy enough to crush a man, and it landed all over him at once, tight all around him.

Before he could react, he felt himself being hoisted high into the air, the net catching him like an animal, its ropes so tight around him that he could not even move, his shoulders and arms and wrists and feet all constrained, crushed together. He was hoisted higher and higher, until he found himself a good twenty feet above the deck, dangling, like an animal caught in a trap.

Erec's heart slammed in his chest as he tried to understand what was going on. He looked down and saw Alistair below him, waking up.

"Alistair!" Erec called out.

Down below, she looked everywhere for him, and when she finally looked up and saw him, her face fell.

"EREC!" she yelled, confused.

Erec watched as several dozen crew members, bearing torches, approached her. They all wore grotesque smiles, evil in their eyes, as they closed in on her.

"It's about time he shared her," one of them said.

"I'm going to teach this princess what it means to live with a sailor!" another said

The group broke into laughter.

"After me," another one said.

"Not before I've had my fill first," another said.

Erec struggled to break free with all that he had as they continued to close in on her. But it was to no avail. His shoulders and arms were clamped so tightly, he could not even wiggle them.

"ALISTAIR!" he screamed, desperate.

He was helpless to do anything but watch as he dangled above.

Three sailors suddenly pounced on Alistair from behind; Alistair screamed out as they pulled her to her feet, tore her shirt, yanked her arms behind her back. They held her tight as several more sailors approached.

Erec scanned the ship for any sign of the captain; he saw him on the upper deck, looking down, watching all of it.

"Captain!" Erec yelled. "This is your ship. Do something!"

The captain looked at him, then slowly turned his back on the whole scene, as if not wanting to watch it.

Erec watched, desperate, as a sailor pulled a knife and held it to Alistair's throat, and Alistair cried out.

"NO!" Erec yelled.

It was like watching a nightmare unfold beneath him—and worst of all, there was nothing he could do.

# CHAPTER FIVE

Thorgrin faced Andronicus, the two of them alone in the field of battle, soldiers dead all around them. He raised his sword high and brought it down on Andronicus's chest; as he did, Andronicus dropped his weapons, smiled wide, and reached out to embrace him.

*My son.*

Thor tried to stop his sword slash, but it was too late. The sword cut right through his father, and as Andronicus split in two, Thor felt wracked with grief.

Thor blinked and found himself walking down an endlessly long altar, holding Gwen's hand. He realized it was their wedding procession. They walked toward a blood-red sun, and as Thor looked to both sides, he saw all the seats were empty. He turned to look at Gwen, and as she looked at him, he was terrified as her skin dried out and she became a skeleton, collapsing to dust in his hand. She fell in a pile of ashes at his feet.

Thor found himself standing before his mother's castle. He had somehow crossed the skywalk, and he stood before immense double doors, gold, shining, three times as tall as he. There was no handle, and he reached up and slammed his palms on them until they started to bleed. The sound echoed throughout the world. But no one came to answer.

Thor threw back his head.

"Mother!" he yelled.

Thor sank to his knees, and as he did, the ground turned into mud, and Thor slid down a cliff, falling and falling, flailing through the air, down, hundreds of feet, to a raging ocean below. He held his hands out to the sky, watched his mother's castle disappear from view, and shrieked.

Thor opened his eyes, breathless, the wind brushing his face, and he looked all around, trying to figure out where he was. He looked down and saw an ocean passing by beneath him, at dizzying speed. He looked up and saw he that clutched something rough, and as he heard the great flapping of wings, he realized he was holding on to Mycoples's scales, his hands cold from the nighttime air, his face numb from the gusts of sea wind. Mycoples flew with great speed, her wings ever flapping, and as Thor looked straight ahead, he realized he had fallen asleep on her. They were still flying, as they had been for days now, racing beneath the night sky, underneath a million twinkling red stars.

Thor sighed and wiped the back of his head, which was covered in sweat. He had vowed to stay alert, but it had been so many days, their trek together, flying, searching for the Land of the Druids. Luckily Mycoples, knowing him as well as she did, knew he was asleep and flew steadily, making sure he did not fall off. The two of them had been traveling so long together, they had become like one. As much as Thor missed the Ring, he was thrilled, at least, to be back with his old friend again, just the two of them, traveling the world; he could tell that she, too, was happy to be with him, purring contentedly. He knew that Mycoples would never let anything bad happen to him—and he felt the same way about her.

Thor looked below and examined the foaming, luminescent green waters of the sea; this was a strange and exotic, one he had never seen before, one of the many they had passed on their search. They continued to fly north, ever north, following the pointing arrow on the relic he had found in his hometown. Thor felt they were getting closer to his mother, to her land, to the Land of the Druids. He could feel it.

Thor hoped that the arrow was accurate. Deep down, he felt it was. He could sense in every fiber of his being that it was taking them closer to his mother, to his destiny.

Thor rubbed his eyes, determined to stay awake. He had thought they would have already found the Land of the Druids by now; it felt as if they had already covered half the world. For moment he worried:

what if it was all a fantasy? What if his mother didn't exist? What if the Land of the Druids didn't exist? What if he was doomed to never find her?

He tried to shake these thoughts from his mind as he urged Mycoples on.

*Faster*, Thor thought.

Mycoples purred and flapped her wings harder, and as she put her head down, the two of them dove into the mist, heading for some point on the horizon that, Thor knew, might not even exist.

*

The day broke as Thor had never seen it, the sky awash with not two suns, but three, all three rising together in different points of the horizon, one red, one green, one purple. They flew just above the clouds, which were spread out beneath him, so close that Thor could touch them, a blanket of color. Thor basked in the most beautiful sunrise he'd ever seen, different colors of the suns breaking through the clouds, the rays streaking over him, beneath him, above him. He felt as if he were flying into the birth of the world.

Thor directed Mycoples down, and he felt moist as they went into the cloud cover; momentarily, his world was awash in different colors, then he was blinded. As they exited the clouds, Thor expected to see yet another ocean, yet another endless expanse of nothingness.

But this time, there was something else.

Thor's heart raced as he spotted beneath them a sight he'd always hoped to see, a sight which occupied his dreams. There, far below, a land came into view. It was an island, swirling in mist, in the midst of this incredible ocean, wide and deep. His relic vibrated, and he looked down and saw the arrow flashing, pointing straight down. But he did not even need to see it to know. He felt it, in every fiber of his being. She was here. His mother. The magical Land of the Druids existed, and he had arrived.

*Down, my friend*, Thor thought.

Mycoples aimed downward, and as they got closer, the island came increasingly into view. Thor saw endless fields of flowers,

33

remarkably similar to the fields he'd seen in King's Court. He could not understand it. The island felt so familiar, almost as if he had arrived back at home. He had expected the land to be more exotic. It was strange how uncannily familiar it was. How could it be?

The island was encased by a vast beach of sparkling red sand, waves crashing against it. As they neared, Thor saw something that surprised him: there appeared to be an entrance to the island, two massive pillars soaring up to the heavens, the tallest pillars he had ever seen, disappearing into the clouds. A wall, perhaps twenty feet high, enclosed the entire island, and passing through these pillars appeared to be the only way to enter on foot.

Since he was on Mycoples, Thor decided he didn't need to go through the pillars. He would just fly over the wall and land on the island, anywhere he wanted. After all, he was not on foot.

Thor directed Mycoples to fly over the wall, but as she got closer, suddenly, she surprised him. She screeched and pulled back sharply, raising her talons in the air until she was nearly vertical. She stopped short, as if slamming into an invisible shield, and Thor held on for dear life. Thor directed her to keep flying, but she would not go any farther.

That's when Thor realized: the island was surrounded by some sort of energy shield, one so powerful that even Mycoples could not pass through. One could not fly over the wall; one had to pass through the pillars, on foot.

Thor directed Mycoples, and they dove down to the red shore. They landed before the pillars, and Thor tried to direct Mycoples to fly between them, through the vast gates, to enter with him into the Land of the Druids.

But again, Mycoples pulled back, raising her talons.

*I cannot enter.*

Thor felt Mycoples's thoughts race through him. He looked at her, saw her closing her huge glowing eyes, blinking, and he understood.

She was telling him that he would have to enter the Land of the Druids alone.

Thor dismounted on the red sand and stood before the pillars, examining them.

"I can't leave you here, my friend," Thor said. "It is too dangerous for you. If I must go alone, then I must go. Return to the safety of home. Wait for me there."

Mycoples shook her head and lowered her head to the ground, lying there, resigned.

*I will wait for you to the ends of the earth.*

Thor could see that she was determined to stay. He knew she was stubborn, that she would not budge.

Thor leaned forward, stroked Mycoples's scales on her long nose, leaned over, and kissed her. She purred, lifted her head, and rested it on his chest.

"I will return for you, my friend," Thor said.

Thor turned and faced the pillars, solid gold, shining in the sun and nearly blinding him, and he took the first step. He felt alive in a way he never thought he would as he passed through the gates, and, finally, into the Land of the Druids.

## CHAPTER SIX

Gwendolyn rode in the back of the carriage, jostling along the country road, leading the expedition of people that wound its way slowly west, away from King's Court. Gwendolyn was pleased with the evacuation, which had been orderly thus far, and pleased with the progress her people had made. She hated leaving her city behind, but she was confident at least that they'd gained enough distance for her people to be safe, to be well on their way to her ultimate mission: to cross the Western Crossing of the Canyon, to board her fleet of ships on the shores of the Tartuvian, and to cross the great ocean for the Upper Isles. It was the only way, she knew, to keep her people safe.

As they marched, thousands of her people on foot all around her, thousands of others jostling in their carts, the sound of horses' hooves filled Gwen's ears, the sound of the steady motion of carts, of humanity. Gwen found herself getting lost in the monotony of the trek, holding Guwayne to her chest, rocking him. Beside her sat Steffen and Illepra, accompanying her the entire way.

Gwendolyn looked out to the road before her and tried to imagine herself anywhere but here. She had worked so hard to rebuild this kingdom, and now here she was, fleeing from it. She was executing her mass evacuation plan because of the McCloud invasion—but more importantly, because of all of the ancient prophecies, of Argon's hints, because of her own dreams and feelings of pending doom. But what if, she wondered, she was wrong? What if it was all just a dream, just worries in the night? What if everything in the Ring would be fine? What if this was an overreaction, an unnecessary evacuation? After all, she could evacuate her people to another city within the Ring, like Silesia. She did not have to take them across an ocean.

Not unless she foresaw a complete and entire destruction of the Ring. Yet from everything she'd read and heard and felt, that

36

destruction was imminent. Evacuation was the only way, she assured herself.

As Gwen looked to the horizon, she wished Thor could be here, at her side. She looked up and scanned the skies, wondering where he was now. Had he found the Land of the Druids? Had he found his mother? Would he return for her?

And would they ever marry?

Gwen looked down into Guwayne's eyes, and she saw Thor looking back at her, saw Thor's grey eyes, and she held her son tighter. She tried not to think of the sacrifice she'd had to make in the Netherworld. Would it all come true? Would the fates be so cruel?

"My lady?"

Gwen started at the voice; she turned and looked to see Steffen, turning in the cart, pointing up to the sky. She noticed that all around her, her people were stopping, and she suddenly felt her own carriage jostled to a halt. She was puzzled as to why the driver would stop without her command.

Gwen followed Steffen's finger, and there, on the horizon, she was shocked to see three arrows shot up high into the air, all aflame, rising, then arching downward, falling to the ground like shooting stars. She was shocked: three arrows aflame could mean only one thing: it was the sign of the MacGils. The claws of the falcon, used to signal victory. It was a sign used by her father and his father before him, a sign meant only for the MacGils. There was no mistaking it: it meant the MacGils had won. They had taken back King's Court.

But how was it possible? she wondered. When they'd left, there was no hope of victory, much less survival, her precious city overrun by McClouds, with no one left to stand guard.

Gwen spotted, on the distant horizon, a banner being raised, higher and higher. She squinted, and again there was no mistake: it was the banner of the MacGils. It could only mean that King's Court was now back in the hands of the MacGils.

On the one hand, Gwen felt elated, and wanted to return at once. On the other hand, as she looked at the road they had traveled, she thought of all Argon's predictions, of the scrolls she had read, of her

37

own premonitions. She felt, deep down, that her people still needed to be evacuated. Perhaps the MacGils had recaptured King's Court; but that did not mean that the Ring was safe. Gwendolyn still felt certain that something much worse was coming, and that she had to get her people out of here, to safety.

"It seems we have won," Steffen said.

"A cause for celebration!" Aberthol called out, approaching her cart.

"King's Court is ours again!" called out a commoner.

A great cheer arose amongst her people.

"We must turn back immediately!" called out another.

Another cheer rose up. But Gwen shook her head adamantly. She stood and faced her people, and all eyes turned to her.

"We shall not turn back!" she boomed to her people. "We have begun the evacuation, and we must stick to it. I know that a great danger lies ahead for the Ring. I must get you to safety while we still have time, while there is still a chance."

Her people groaned, dissatisfied, and several commoners stepped forward, pointing to the horizon.

"I don't know about the rest of you," one bellowed, "but King's Court is my home! It is everything I know and love! I'm not about to cross the sea to some strange island while our city is intact and in the hands of the MacGils! I'm turning back for King's Court!"

A great cheer rose up, and as he left, walking back, hundreds of people fell in and followed him, turning their carts, heading back down the road toward King's Court.

"My lady, should I stop them?" Steffen asked, panicked, loyal to her to a fault.

"You are hearing the voice of the people, my lady," Aberthol said, coming up beside her. "You would be foolish to deny them. Moreover, you cannot. It is their home. It is all that they know. Do not fight your own people. Do not lead them without good reason."

"But I have good reason," Gwen said. "I know destruction is coming."

Aberthol shook his head.

"And yet they do not," he replied. "I do not doubt you. But queens plan ahead, while the masses act on instinct. And a queen is only as powerful as the masses allow her to be."

Gwen stood there, burning with frustration as she watched her people defy her command, migrating back to King's Court. It was the first time they had ever openly rebelled, had openly defied her. She did not like the feeling. Was it portending things to come? Were her days as queen numbered?

"My lady, shall I command the soldiers to stop them?" Steffen asked.

She felt as if he was the only one left still loyal to her. A part of her wanted to say yes.

But as she watched them go, she knew it would be futile.

"No," she said softly, her voice broken, feeling as if her child had just turned her back on her. What pained her the most was that she knew their actions would only lead to their harm, and there was nothing she could do to stop it. "I cannot prevent what destiny holds for them."

*

Gwendolyn, despondent as she trailed her people in the return to King's Court, rode through the rear gates of King's Court and already heard the distant cheers of celebration coming from the other side. Her people were elated, dancing and cheering, throwing their hats into the air as they all poured through the gates, returning to the courtyards of the city they knew and loved, the city they called home. Everyone rushed to congratulate the Legion, Kendrick, and the victorious Silver.

But Gwendolyn proceeded with a pit in her stomach, torn by mixed feelings. On the one hand, she was of course elated to be back here, too, elated that they had conquered the McClouds, elated to see that Kendrick and the others were safe. She took pride in seeing the McCloud corpses littered all over the place, and she was thrilled to see that her brother Godfrey had managed to survive, sitting off to the side nursing a wound, head in hand.

Yet at the same time, Gwendolyn could not quell her deep sense of foreboding, her certainty that some other terrible calamity was coming for them all, and that the best thing for her people to do was to evacuate before it was too late.

But her people were swept up in victory. They would hear no reason as she was ushered, with thousands of others, into the sprawling city she knew so well. As they entered, Gwen was relieved to see that, at least, the McClouds had been killed quickly, before they'd had a chance to do any real damage to all of her careful rebuilding.

"Gwendolyn!"

Gwendolyn turned to see Kendrick dismount, rush forward, and embrace her. She hugged him back, his armor hard and cold, as she handed Guwayne to Illepra beside her.

"My brother," she said, looking up at him, his eyes shining with victory. "I am proud of you. You've done more than hold our city—you have vanquished our attackers. You and your Silver. You embody our code of honor. Father would be proud."

Kendrick grinned as he bowed his head.

"I am grateful for your words, sister. I was not about to allow your city, our city, father's city, be destroyed by those heathens. I was not alone; you should know that our brother Godfrey put up the first resistance. He and a small handful of others, and even the Legion—they all helped hold back the attackers."

Gwen turned to see Godfrey walking over at them, a beleaguered smile on his face, holding one hand to the side of his head, caked with dried blood.

"You became a man today, my brother," she said to him in earnest, draping a hand on his shoulder. "Father would be proud."

Godfrey smiled back sheepishly.

"I just wanted to warn you," he said.

She smiled.

"You did far more than that."

Alongside him came Elden, O'Connor, Conven, and dozens of Legion members.

"My lady," Elden said. "Our men fought valiantly here today. Yet I'm sad to say, we have lost many."

Gwen looked past him and saw the dead bodies all over King's Court. Thousands of McClouds—yet also dozens of Legion recruits. Even a handful of Silver were dead. It brought back painful memories of the last time her city was invaded. It was hard for Gwen to look.

She turned and saw a dozen McClouds, captives, still alive, heads down, hands behind their backs.

"And who are these?" she asked.

"The McCloud generals," Kendrick replied. "We've kept them alive. They are all that remains of their army. What do you command we do with them?"

Gwendolyn looked them over slowly, staring them in the eye as she did. Each one stared back at her, proud, defiant. Their faces were crude, typical McClouds, never showing remorse.

Gwen sighed. There had been a time when she had thought that peace was the answer to everything, that if only she could be kind enough and gracious enough to her neighbors, could show enough goodwill, then they'd be kind to her and her people.

But the longer she ruled, the more she saw that others only interpreted overtures of peace as a sign of weakness, as something to be taken advantage of. All her efforts at peace had culminated in this: a surprise attack. And on Pilgrimage Day no less, the holiest day of the year.

Gwendolyn felt herself hardening inside. She did not have the same naïveté, the same faith in man, that she once did. More and more, she had faith in only one thing: a reign of steel.

As Kendrick and the others all looked to her, Gwendolyn raised her voice:

"Kill them all," she said.

Their eyes widened in surprise, and respect. They clearly had not expected this from their queen who had always strived for peace.

"Did I hear correctly, my lady?" Kendrick asked, shock in his voice.

Gwendolyn nodded.

"You did," she replied. "When you're done, collect their corpses, and expel them from our gates."

Gwendolyn turned and walked away, through the courtyard of King's Court, and as she did, she heard behind her the screams of the McClouds. Despite herself, she flinched.

Gwen walked through a city filled with corpses and yet filled with cheering and music and dancing, thousands of people swarming back to their homes, refilling the city as if nothing bad had ever happened. As she watched them, her heart filled with dread.

"The city is ours again," Kendrick said, coming up beside her.

Gwendolyn shook her head.

"Just for a short while."

He looked at her in surprise.

"What do you mean?"

She stopped and faced him.

"I've seen the prophecies," she said. "The ancient scripts. I've spoken with Argon. I've dreamt a dream. An attack is coming our way. It was a mistake to return here. We must all evacuate at once."

Kendrick looked at her, his face ashen, and Gwen sighed as she surveyed her people.

"But my people will not listen."

Kendrick shook his head.

"What if you're mistaken?" he said. "What if you are looking too deeply into prophecies? We have the finest fighting army in the world. Nothing can reach our gates. The McClouds are dead, and we have no other enemies left in the Ring. The Shield is up and holds strong. And we also have Ralibar, wherever he is. You have nothing to fear. *We* have nothing to fear."

Gwendolyn shook her head.

"That is precisely the moment when you have the most to fear," she replied.

Kendrick sighed.

"My lady, this was just a freak attack," he said. "They surprised us on Pilgrimage Day. We shall never leave King's Court unguarded

42

again. This city is a fortress. It has held for thousands of years. There is no one left to topple us."

"You are wrong," she said.

"Well, even if I am, you see that the people won't leave. My sister," Kendrick said, his voice softening, imploring, "I love you. But I speak as your commander. As the commander of the Silver. If you try to force your people to evacuate, to do what they do not want to do, you will have a revolt on your hands. They do not see whatever danger that you do. And to be honest, I do not even see it myself."

Gwendolyn looked at her people, and she knew that Kendrick was right. They would not listen to her. Even her own brother did not believe her.

And it broke her heart.

*

Gwendolyn stood alone on the upper parapets of her castle, holding Guwayne tight and looking out at the sunset, the two suns hanging low in the sky. Down below, she heard the muted shouts and celebrations of her people, all preparing for a huge night of celebration. Out there, she saw the rolling vistas of the lands surrounding King's Court, a kingdom at its peak. Everywhere was the bounty of summer, endless fields of green, orchards, a lush land rich with bounty. The land was content, rebuilt after so much tragedy, and she saw a world at peace with itself.

Gwendolyn furrowed her brow, wondering how any sort of darkness could ever reach here. Maybe the darkness she had imagined had already come in the form of the McClouds. Maybe it had already been averted, thanks to Kendrick and the others. Maybe Kendrick had been right. Maybe she had grown too cautious since she had become Queen, had seen too much tragedy. Maybe she was, like Kendrick said, looking too deeply into things.

After all, to evacuate her people from their homes, to lead them across the Canyon, onto ships, to the volatile Upper Isles, was a drastic move, a move reserved for a time of the greatest calamity. What if she did so, and no tragedy ever befell the Ring? She'd be known as the Queen who panicked with no danger in sight.

Gwendolyn sighed, clutching Guwayne as he squirmed in her arms, and wondered if she were losing her mind. She looked up and searched the skies for any sign of Thorgrin, hoping, praying. At least, she hoped for any sign of Ralibar, wherever he was. But he, too, had not returned.

Gwen watched an empty sky, once again disappointed. Once again, she would have to rely on herself. Even her people, who had always supported her, who had looked to her as a god, now seemed to distrust her. Her father had never prepared her for this. Without the support of her people, what sort of Queen would she be? Powerless.

Gwen desperately wanted to turn to someone for comfort, for answers. But Thorgrin was gone; her mother was gone; seemingly everyone she knew and loved was gone. She felt at a crossroads, and had never felt more confused.

Gwen closed her eyes and called upon God to help her. She tried with all her will to summon him. She had never been one to pray much, but her faith was strong, and she felt certain that he existed.

*Please, God. I am so confused. Show me how to best protect my people. Show me how to best protect Guwayne. Show me how to be a great ruler.*

"Prayers are a powerful thing," came a voice.

Gwen spun at once, instantly relieved to hear that voice. Standing there, several feet away, was Argon. He was clothed in his white cloak and hood, holding his staff, looking out at the horizon instead of her.

"Argon, I need answers. Please. Help me."

"We are always in need of answers," he replied. "And yet they do not always come. Our lives are meant to be lived out. The future cannot always be told for us."

"But it can be hinted at," Gwendolyn said. "All the prophecies I've read, all the scrolls, the history of the Ring—still point to a great darkness that is coming. You must tell me. Will it occur?"

Argon turned and stared at her, his eyes filled with fire, darker and scarier than she'd ever seen them.

"Yes," he replied.

The definiteness of his answer scared her more than anything. He, Argon, who always spoke in riddles.

Gwen shivered inside.

"Will it come here, to King's Court?"

"Yes," he replied.

Gwen felt her sense of dread deepening. She also felt secure in her conviction that she had been right all along.

"Will the Ring will be destroyed?" she asked.

Argon looked to her, and nodded slowly.

"There are but a few things left that I can tell you," he said. "If you choose, this can be one of them."

Gwen thought long and hard. She knew Argon's wisdom was precious. Yet this was something she really needed to know.

"Tell me," she said.

Argon took a deep breath as he turned and surveyed the horizon for what felt like forever.

"The Ring will be destroyed. Everything you know and love will be wiped away. The place you now stand will be nothing but flaming embers and ashes. All of the Ring will be ashes. Your nation will be gone. A darkness is coming. A darkness greater than any darkness in our history."

Gwendolyn felt the truth of his words reverberate inside her, felt the deep timbre of his voice resonate to her very core. She knew that every word he spoke was true.

"My people do not see this," she said, her voice shaking.

Argon shrugged.

"You are Queen. Sometimes force must be used. Not only against one's enemies. But even against one's people. Do what you know. Do not always seek your people's approval. Approval is an elusive thing. Sometimes, when your people hate you the most, that is a sign that you are doing the best thing for them. Your father was blessed with a reign of peace. But you, Gwendolyn, you will have a far greater test: you will have a reign of steel."

As Argon turned to walk away, Gwendolyn stepped forward and reached out for him.

"Argon," she called.

He stopped, but did not turn around.

45

"Just tell me one more thing. I beg you. Will I ever see Thorgrin again?"

He paused, a long, heavy silence. In that grim silence, she felt her heart breaking in two, hoping and praying that he would give her just one more answer.

"Yes," he replied.

She stood there, her heart pounding, craving more.

"Can you tell me nothing more?"

He turned and looked at her, sadness in his eyes.

"Remember the choice you made. Not every love is meant to last forever."

High above, Gwen heard a falcon screech, and she looked to the sky, wondering.

She turned to look back at Argon, but he was already gone.

She clutched Guwayne tight and looked out at her kingdom, taking one long last look, wanting to remember it like this, when it was still vibrant, alive. Before it all turned to ash. She wondered with dread what danger so great could be lurking beyond that veneer of beauty. She shuddered, as she knew, without a doubt, that it would find them all very soon.

# CHAPTER SEVEN

Stara yelled as she plummeted through the air, flailing, Reece beside her, Matus and Srog beside him, the four of them falling from the castle wall in the blinding wind and rain, plunging toward the ground. She braced herself as she saw the large bushes come up at her quickly, and she realized the only reason she might survive this fall was because of them.

A moment later, Stara felt as if every bone in her body was breaking as she smashed into the bush—which barely broke her fall—and continued on until she hit the ground. She felt the wind knocked out of her, and was sure she bruised a rib. Yet at the same time, she sank several inches and realized the ground was softer, muddier than she thought, and cushioned her fall.

The others hit, too, beside her, and all of them began to tumble as the mud gave way. Stara hadn't anticipated they would land on a steep slope, and before she could stop herself, she was sliding with the others, rushing downhill, all of them caught up in a mudslide.

They rolled and slid, and soon the gushing waters carried them, sliding down the mountain at full speed. As she slid, Stara looked back over her shoulder and saw her father's castle quickly fading from view, and realized that at least it was taking them away, far from their attackers.

Stara looked back down and dodged as she narrowly avoided rocks in her path, going so fast she could hardly catch her breath. The mud was unbelievably slick, and the rain came down harder, her world spinning at lightning speed. She tried to slow, grasping at the mud, but it was impossible.

Just as Stara wondered if this would ever end, she was flooded with panic as she remembered where this slope led: right off the side of a cliff. If they didn't stop themselves soon, she realized, they would all be dead.

Stara saw that none of the others could stop the slide either, all of them flailing, groaning, trying their hardest but helpless. Stara looked out and saw, with dread, the drop-off fast approaching. With no way to stop themselves, they were about to go right over the edge.

Suddenly Stara saw Srog and Matus veer to the left, to a small cave perched at the edge of the precipice. They somehow managed to smash into the rocks feet first, coming to a standstill just before they went over the edge.

Stara tried to dig her heels into the mud, but nothing was working; she merely spun and tumbled, and seeing the precipice coming up on her, she yelled, knowing she'd be over the edge in a second.

Suddenly, Stara felt a rough hand grabbing the back of her shirt, slowing her speed, then stopping her. She looked up to see Reece. He clung to a flimsy tree, one arm wrapped around it, at the edge of the precipice, his other hand reaching out and holding her as water and mud gushed, pulling her away. She was losing ground, nearly dangling over the edge. He had stopped her fall, but she was losing ground.

Reece could not continue to hold her, and she knew that if he didn't let go, soon they would both go over together. They would both die.

"Let me go!" she yelled up at him.

But he shook his head adamantly.

"Never!" he yelled back, his face dripping with water, over the rain.

Reece suddenly let go of the tree so he could reach out and grab her wrists with both hands; at the same time, he wrapped his legs around the tree, holding himself from behind. He yanked her to him with all his might, his legs the only thing keeping them both from going over.

With one final move, he groaned and cried and managed to yank her out of the current, to the side, and sent her rolling over to the cave with the others. Reece tumbled with her as she went, rolling out of the current himself, and helping her as she crawled.

48

When they reached the safety of the cave Stara collapsed, exhausted, lying face-first in the mud, and so grateful to be alive.

As she lay there, breathing hard, dripping wet, she wondered not about how close she'd come to death, but rather about one thing: did Reece still love her? She realized she cared more about that than even whether or not she lived.

\*

Stara sat huddled around the small fire inside the cave, the others close by, finally starting to dry off. She looked around and realized the four of them looked like survivors of a war, cheeks sunken, all staring into the flames, holding up their hands and rubbing them, trying to shelter themselves from the ceaseless wet and cold. They listened to the wind and rain, the ever-present elements of the Upper Isles, thrashing outside. It felt like it would never end.

It was night now, and they had waited all day to light this fire, for fear of being seen. Finally, they had all been so cold and tired and miserable, they had risked it. Stara felt enough time had passed from their escape—and besides, there was no way those men would dare to venture all the way down to these cliffs. It was too steep and wet, and if they did, they would die trying.

Still, the four of them were trapped in here, like prisoners. If they stepped foot outside the cave, eventually an army of Upper Islanders would find them, and kill them all. Her brother would have no mercy on her, either. It was hopeless.

She sat near a distant, brooding Reece, and pondered the events. She had saved Reece's life back in the fort, but he had saved hers on the cliff. Did he still care for her the way he once did? The way that she still cared for him? Or was he still bitter over what had happened to Selese? Did he blame her? Would he ever forgive her?

Stara could not imagine the pain he was going through as he sat there, head in his hands, staring into the fire like a man who was lost. She wondered what was racing through his mind. He looked like a man with nothing left to lose, like a man who had been to the edge of suffering and had not quite returned. A man wracked by guilt. He did not look like the man she had once known, the man so full of love and joy, so quick to smile, who'd showered her with love and affection. Now, instead, he looked as if something had died inside of him.

Stara looked up, afraid to meet Reece's eyes, yet needing to see his face. She hoped secretly that he would be staring at her, thinking of her. Yet when she saw him, her heart broke to see that he was not looking at her at all. Instead, he just stared into the flames, the loneliest look on his face that she had ever seen.

Stara could not help wondering for the millionth time if whatever had existed between them was over, ruined by Selese's death. For the millionth time, she cursed her brothers—and her father—for putting into action such a devious plot. She had always wanted Reece to herself, of course; but she would never have condoned the subterfuge that had led to her demise. She had never wanted Selese to die, or even to be hurt. She had hoped that Reece would break the news to her in a gentle way, and that while upset, she would understand—and certainly not take her own life. Or destroy Reece's.

Now all of Stara's plans, her entire future, had crumbled before her eyes, thanks to her awful family. Matus was the only rational one left of her bloodline. Yet Stara wondered what would become of him, of the four of them. Would they just rot and die here in this cave? Eventually they would have to leave it. And her brother's men, she knew, were relentless. He would not stop until he'd killed them all—especially after Reece had killed her father.

Stara knew she should feel some remorse at her father being dead—and yet she felt none at all. She hated the man, and always had. If anything, she felt relieved, even grateful to Reece for killing him. He had been a lying, honorless warrior and king his entire life, and no father to her at all.

Stara glanced at these three warriors, all sitting there looking distraught. They'd been silent for hours, and she wondered if any them had a plan. Srog was badly wounded, and Matus and Reece had been wounded as well, though their injuries were minor. They all looked frozen to the bone, beaten down by the weather of this place, by the odds against them.

"So are we all going to sit in this cave forever, and die here?" Stara asked, breaking the thick silence, no longer able to stand the monotony or the gloom.

Slowly, Srog and Matus looked over at her. But Reece still would not look up and meet her eyes.

"And where would you have us go?" Srog asked, defensive. "The entire island is crawling with your brother's men. What chance do we hold against them? Especially with them enraged at our escape and your father's death."

"You got us into a pickle, my cousin," Matus said, smiling, putting a hand on Reece's shoulder. "That was a bold act of yours. Possibly the boldest act I've seen in my life."

Reece shrugged.

"He stole my bride. He deserved to die."

Stara bristled at the word *bride*. It broke her heart. His choice of that word told her everything—clearly, Reece was still in love with Selese. He would not even meet Stara's eyes. She felt like crying.

"Do not worry, cousin," Matus said. "I rejoice my father is dead, and I am glad that you are the one who killed him. I do not blame you. I admire you. Even if you nearly got us all killed in the process."

Reece nodded, clearly appreciating Matus's words.

"But no one answered me," Stara said. "What is the plan? For us all to die here?"

"What is *your* plan?" Reece shot back at her.

"I have none," she said. "I did my part. I rescued us all from that place."

"Yes, you did," Reece admitted, still looking into the flames rather than at her. "I owe you my life."

Stara felt a glimmer of hope at Reece's words, even if he would still not meet her eyes. She wondered if maybe he did not hate her after all.

"And you saved mine," she replied. "From the edge of the cliff. We are even."

51

Reece still stared into to the flames.

She waited for him to say something back, to say that he loved her, to say anything. But he said nothing. Stara found herself reddening.

"Is that it then?" she said. "Have we nothing else to say to each other? Is our business done?"

Reece raised his head, meeting her eyes for the first time with a puzzled expression.

Stara could stand it no more. She jumped to her feet and stormed away from the others, standing at the edge of the cave, her back to all of them. She looked out at the night, the rain, the wind, and she wondered: was everything over between her and Reece? If it was, she felt no reason to go on living.

"We can escape to the ships," Reece finally said, after an interminable silence, his terse words cutting through the night.

Stara turned and looked at him.

"Escape to the ships?" she asked.

Reece nodded.

"Our men are down there, in the harbor below. We must go to them. It is the last MacGil territory left in this place."

Stara shook her head.

"A reckless plan," she said. "The ships will be surrounded, if they have not already been destroyed. We'd have to get through all of my brother's men to get there. Better to hide out somewhere else on the island."

Reece shook his head, determined.

"No," he said. "Those are *our* men. We must go to them, whatever the cost. If they are attacked, then we will go down fighting with them."

"You don't seem to understand," she said, equally determined. "At morning light, thousands of my brother's men will litter the shores. There is no way past them."

Reece stood, brushing off the dampness, a fire in his eyes.

"Then we shall not wait for morning light," he said. "We will go now. Before the sun rises."

Matus slowly stood, too, and Reece looked down at Srog.

"Srog?" Matus asked. "Can you make it?"

Srog grimaced as he stumbled to his feet, Matus lending a hand.

"I will not hold you back," Srog said. "Go without me. I will stay here in this cave."

"You will die here in this cave," Matus said.

"Well then you will not die with me," he replied.

Reece shook his head.

"*No man left behind*," he said. "You will join us, no matter what it takes."

Reece, Matus, and Srog walked up beside Stara at the edge of the cave, gazing out into the howling wind and rain. Stara looked the three men over, wondering if they were crazy.

"You wanted a plan," Reece said, turning to her. "Well, now we have one."

She shook her head slowly.

"Reckless," she said. "That is the way of men. We will likely die on the way to the ships."

Reece shrugged.

"We will all die one day anyway."

As they all stood there, watching the elements, waiting for that perfect moment, Stara waited for Reece to do something, anything, to take her hand, to show her, even in the smallest way, that he still cared for her.

But he did not. He kept his hand to himself and Stara felt herself hardening, crushed inside. She prepared to embark, no longer caring what fate had in store for her. As they all stepped out into the darkness together, she realized that, without Reece's love, she had nothing left to lose.

# CHAPTER EIGHT

Alistair stood on the ship, terrified, arms bound behind her, her heart pounding as dozens of sailors closed in on her from all sides, a look of lust and death in their eyes. She realized that these men all aimed to rape and torture and kill her, and that they would take delight in doing so. She marveled that such evil existed in the world, and for a moment she struggled to understand humankind.

Her entire life, she'd always been known, everywhere she went, as the most beautiful girl—and more than once it had gotten her into trouble. She just wanted to be left alone. She had always just wanted to look normal, like everybody else. She never wanted to attract attention—and she certainly did not want to attract trouble.

Erec, swinging high overhead in the net, shouted down, helpless, infuriated.

"ALISTAIR!" he yelled again and again, trying frantically to squirm out.

The sailors below laughed, taking great delight in his capture, and his helplessness.

Alistair looked at them and felt a great anger; she forced herself to be bold, fearless.

"Why would you want to hurt me?" she asked, her voice filled with compassion. "Don't you see that your behavior only harms you? We are all part of the same planet."

The men laughed in her face.

"Fancy words from a stupid girl!" one of them yelled, as he reached up a big beefy palm, swung it high, and prepared to smack her across the face.

As he lowered his hands toward her, something strange happened to Alistair. A sensation came over her, one she'd never experienced: it was as if the entire world slowed down, the man's hand moving at a snail's pace in midair. As she focused on it, it seemed to freeze. The

54

entire world seemed to freeze. She saw every particle in fine detail, saw the very fiber of nature in the spirit and souls of these men.

Alistair suddenly felt a surge of energy. She felt herself on a different realm, able to transcend everything before her, able to have power over it all through sympathy and love and compassion. She felt a tremendous strength rise within her, a strength which she herself could not even understand. It felt like the power of a thousand suns coursing through her veins.

Alistair blinked, and the world came back to life again in a great flash of light. She looked up at the man's hand, still frozen in midair, and he suddenly became panicked with fear as he looked at his own hand, unable to move it. He looked back and forth from Alistair to his hand, shocked.

"A sorcerer!" he exclaimed.

Alistair stood there, unafraid, sensing the power of a greater spirit within her, and sensing that these men, of a different spiritual plane, could not touch her. She felt swept up in a power and force in the world greater than she.

Alistair leaned back and raised her hands up to the heavens, and as she did, beams of white light streamed from her palms, shooting straight up, lighting up the night, piercing through the heavens, to the black night itself.

Suddenly, the ship rocked wildly from side to side. The howling of the wind picked up, and great waves rose up all around the ship, a huge current, rocking the ship violently, up and down.

All the men facing her were thrown to the deck, and as the ship listed, they went sliding, all the way, until they slammed into the wooden side. The ship rocked the other way, and the men slid all the way to the other end, smashing into that side, groaning in pain. Alistair stood with two feet rooted to the deck, and she felt like a mountain, keeping perfect balance, feeling centered in the very core of the world.

The ship rocked again, and the men slid the other way, shouting out as they smashed into the sides of the ship, again and again and again, until their ribs were cracked.

As the men slid one more time, the ship nearly on its side, they shrieked in terror as they looked out over the edge: there arose an immense splashing noise, as though the very bowels of the ocean were shooting to the surface, and an enormous sea monster emerged from the depths. It was twice as large as a great whale, with a wide, flat head, shiny red scales, and thousands of razor-sharp teeth. Its body was thicker than the ship, and it rose straight up out of the waters with a great fury, and let out a shriek so violent, it nearly split the mast in two. The men clutched their ears, trying to drown out the sound, but even so, many of their ears ran with blood.

The whale rose entirely out of the water, larger than a dragon, larger than anything Alistair had ever seen, and then it dove, face first, straight down onto the ship, its jaws wide open.

The men raised their arms and screamed. But it was too late; the whale's teeth came straight down, through half of the ship, and tore it to pieces. He scooped up the men, their blood streaming from its teeth as it closed its jaw, and then disappeared just as quickly, sucking them back down beneath the ocean.

The ship, now empty, destroyed, was sinking fast, and Alistair looked up to see Erec, swinging back and forth in his net. She watched as the rope snapped and he came crashing down onto the deck. Erec used his dagger to slice open the net and free himself. He scrambled to his feet and ran to her.

They embraced.

"Alistair," he said. "Thank god you're safe."

The ship was taking on water fast. Over the sound of the wind and the waves came the shouts of men, and Alistair turned and saw the captain; he came running down from the upper decks, along with dozens more sailors from the back of the ship.

"There!" Erec shouted.

Alistair turned and followed his finger to see a small vessel, a twenty-foot rowboat with a small sail, attached by ropes to the side of the ship, clearly the lifeboat to this huge vessel. The sailors were racing for it, and Erec grabbed her hand and they ran across the deck, getting a good head start on the others.

They reached the lifeboat first, and Erec lifted Alistair and put her in the little boat as the ship rocked; she grabbed hold of the rope, trying to steady herself.

"Don't you touch our boat!" the captain screamed.

Erec wheeled, and as the captain approached, Erec stabbed him in the heart with his sword. The captain gasped and dropped to his knees, eyes bulging in shock, as Erec stood over him, grimacing.

"I should have done that long ago," Erec said.

Several more sailors approached, and Erec, unleashed, fought with a vengeance, slashing and killing a dozen of them as they lamely raised their swords and tried to fight back. They were no match for him.

"Erec, we must go!" Alistair called out, as the ship lurched.

The ship rocked violently, taking on even more water, as dozens more sailors began to run toward him. Erec turned and jumped into the rowboat, and as soon as he did, he cut the ropes.

Alistair felt her heart in her throat as they plummeted through the air, down into the ocean, hitting the waves with a great splash, rocking and rolling as the ocean tossed and turned.

They escaped just in time; a moment later, the huge ship reeled sideways, turning over. The sailors who remained on board shrieked with their last breaths as the ocean sucked them under, along with the ship, in a great cracking of wood.

Erec rowed with all his might, distancing them from the ship, and soon, the screams quieted. Soon, it was just the two of them, sailing into the black of night, under a million red stars, heading God knew where in the universe.

# CHAPTER NINE

Thor walked through the Land of the Druids, in awe at his surroundings, at once so exotic and yet so eerily familiar. As he traversed a field of flowers, he reached out and touched them in wonder, trying to understand where he had seen them before, where he had seen this entire vista before. The more he examined it, the more he began to remember: it was a field of flowers he had been to before. The field outside King's Court. The place where he had his first date with Gwendolyn. It had been a magical place for him, a place burned into his memory, where he had first fallen in love. A place he could never forget.

But what could it possibly be doing here, halfway across the world, in the Land of the Druids? Had he crossed the world only to return home? It made no sense.

As Thor walked, deeper into the field, he struggled to understand what was happening. He felt his entire body tingling, and he sensed from the feeling that he was indeed in a different land, a different place. A different energy hung in the air, a different weight and scent to the breeze. For the first time in his life, Thor felt as if the energy aligned with his own perfectly. As if he were home, among his people. People who were like him. People who understood him. He felt more alive, stronger here, than anywhere else in the world.

Yet the same time, his surroundings also felt different, foreign to him. He sensed a foreboding, a danger, and he did not know what.

Thor searched the horizon, hoping to see something familiar—the towering castle of his dreams, his mother's palace, the skywalk leading to it—or at the very least, some path leading to it.

But he saw none of that. Instead, as he traversed the field of flowers, following a meandering dirt path, the landscape suddenly gave way to a small village, the dirt path cutting through it, filled with white stone cottages.

Thor held his breath, shocked, as the hairs rose on his arms: it was *his* town. His home village.

How as it possible? he wondered. Had he traveled half the world only to end up back home?

Thor continued to walk, warily, through the empty streets, until up ahead, he saw a figure in the distance. The figure was hunched over on the side of the dirt path, and as Thor approached he was surprised to see it was an old woman, hunched over a cauldron above a fire. She seemed familiar too.

She looked up at him and grimaced.

"Careful where you step!" she scolded.

Thor recognized that voice, and suddenly he remembered: it was the old woman from his village, the one always hunched over her stew, always yelling at him as he ran by, disturbing her chickens. Was he seeing things?

"What are you doing here?" he asked, dumbfounded.

"The question is: what are you doing here?"

Thor blinked, confused.

"I've come to find my mother."

"Have you? And how do you plan to do that?"

Thor looked down at his relic and saw that the arrow was no longer pointing in any direction. It had shattered. He had arrived, and yet now that he was here, he was on his own. He had no idea how to find her now.

Thor stared back at the woman.

"I don't know," he finally answered. "How big is the Land of the Druids?"

The old woman threw her head back and cackled, an awful, grating sound that sent shivers up his spine.

Finally, she said: "I can tell you where she is."

Thor looked at her in surprise.

"You can? But how would you know?"

She stirred her cauldron.

"For a price," she said, "I will tell you anything."

"What price?" Thor asked.

"Your bracelet."

Thor looked down at his bracelet, the golden one that Alistair had given him, shining in the light. He hesitated. He sensed it had tremendous power, and he felt it was the only thing protecting him here in this land. He had a premonition that, if he gave it to her, he would lose all of his strength.

Then again, Thor needed to know where his mother was.

"It is a gift," he said. "I am sorry. I cannot."

The woman shrugged.

"Then I cannot help you."

Thor looked at her in wonder, frustrated.

"Please," he said. "I need your help."

She stirred her cauldron for a long time, then finally she sighed.

"Look into my cauldron. What do you see?"

Thor looked at her, confused, then finally glanced down at her cauldron.

He blinked several times, caught off guard, and leaned in closer, trying to get a good look.

In the still waters, slowly, a reflection emerged. At first it looked like his face; but then, slowly, he realized it was not his face. It was the face of Andronicus.

Thor looked at the woman, who stared back, evil.

"Who are you?" he asked.

She smiled wide at him.

"I am everyone," she said. "And no one."

She jumped up from her cauldron, reached up and snatched the bracelet off his wrist. As Thor reached out to grab it back, she suddenly transformed before his eyes, morphing into a long, thick white snake. Thor watched with horror and realized it was a deadly Whiteback, the same snake he'd spotted on his first date with Gwendolyn. The sign of death.

The snake grew longer and longer, and before Thor could react, its tail wrapped around his ankles, then around his shins, knees, thighs, waist, and chest. It constricted his arms, and he stood there, barely able to breathe as it crushed him.

60

The snake then leaned back all the way and opened its fangs wide, and Thor turned his face, feeling its hot breath on his neck and knowing that, in moments, it would sink its fangs into his throat.

# CHAPTER TEN

Romulus marched across the southern province of the Ring, watching with glee as his tens of thousands of men charged forward for the gates of Savaria. Hundreds of citizens of the Ring streamed for the city gates, and the knights standing guard lowered the huge iron portcullis and slammed it shut with a bang, just as the last person entered. They raised the drawbridge over the moat, and Romulus watched, and smiled wider. These Savarians really thought they could keep him out. They had no idea what was coming for them.

Romulus heard a great cry, and he looked overhead to see his host of dragons come flying, circling above, awaiting his command. He raised his fist and lowered it, and as he did, they dove forward, racing for the horizon. For Savaria.

The dragons flew over the massive walls, over the city gates, as if they did not even exist, and as they came close to the ground, they breathed a wall of fire.

Screams of thousands arose behind the city walls, helpless civilians slaughtered by the dragons' breath, burned alive, trying to run, with nowhere to go. He watched through the iron gates as knights raised their swords uselessly, their weapons melting in their hands, down to their wrists, their very armor melting on them, screaming as they, too, were burned alive.

No one was safe from the dragons' wrath. The great walls, meant to keep invaders out, instead kept the waves of dragon fire in, creating a fishbowl effect. Even one dragon could have laid waste to the city. Dozens of them rained down an apocalypse.

Romulus breathed deeply and took great satisfaction in the hell before him. He beamed, riding slowly on his horse, as he felt the heat from the waves of fire. Fire scorched the city walls, flames licking higher and higher, pouring out through the windows, like a huge blazing cauldron that could not be quenched.

Romulus's men stopped at the edge of the moat, unable to go any closer because of the intense heat. They waited and waited, until finally Romulus raised his hand, and the dragons fell back, returning, circling again over his head.

The flames finally subsided, and as they did, Romulus's men rushed forward and lowered a long wooden makeshift bridge over the moat. The first battalion raced over it, holding a long iron pole, and they rammed the iron portcullis, still in flames. Sparks flew everywhere, as they rammed it again and again; finally, it caved in, amidst a great cloud of flame and sparks, revealing a wall of flame behind it.

They all stood there waiting, as Romulus directed his horse slowly toward the front line. Behind him, seated on his horse, was his prize, his new plaything—Luanda—her wrists and hands bound, her mouth gagged, her ankles tied to the saddle. She had been forced to ride with him. He could have killed her, of course, but he much preferred to prolong her hell, to make her witness what he was about to do to her homeland. There was something about her, something defiant and evil, he was starting to like, and he wondered if she might even be an appropriate mate for him.

Romulus stopped as he reached the edge of the moat, then gave a terse nod. Hundreds of his men, awaiting his command, burst into the city with a great shout and a sound of horns, and soon the city was filled with his men. He watched with pride as the banner of the Empire was hoisted above its gates.

Savaria, he knew, was one of the great cities of the Ring. And now, every person within, in a matter of minutes, every knight and soldier and commoner and lord, lay dead. And he had not lost a single soldier. It had been the same for his entire march from the Canyon, Romulus slowly and meticulously wiping out every town and village that he encountered, wanting his destruction of the Ring to be absolute.

Of course, King's Court was still free, but he wanted to take his time before arriving there. He wanted everything destroyed first, not a blade of grass left, as vengeance for his prior defeat. He would reach

Gwendolyn in good time, and her King's Court. He would unleash his dragons, and he would make her pay. But not before he had first destroyed every town in her precious Ring.

Romulus threw back his head and roared with triumph. For however long the spell lasted, he was invincible. And as long as he lived, nothing, and no one, in the world would stop him.

# CHAPTER ELEVEN

Gwendolyn rode on the back of Ralibar, hanging on for dear life, wondering how she got here. Ralibar flew erratically, unlike he ever had before, weaving up and down, racing through the clouds, as if wanting her off.

"Ralibar, please, slow!" she cried out.

But Ralibar would not listen. He was like a different beast, a dragon she did not know. He roared—a terrifying noise—and dove straight down through the clouds—right, Gwen saw, for King's Court.

"I can't hang on!" Gwen yelled, slipping.

But Ralibar flew faster, steeper, and a moment later, Gwen shrieked as she lost her grip.

Gwen went tumbling through the air, head over heels, flying straight down toward King's Court. And Ralibar, instead of swooping down to catch her, flew off, away from her.

Gwendolyn braced herself, shrieking, as the ground rushed up for her.

She landed hard on a floor of mud, feeling the pain in every part of her body. Yet also alive.

Gwen got up slowly, wondering how she could have survived. She looked all around and barely recognized King's Court. It was all in ruins, and she lay in the center of it, the only person left alive.

She heard a baby's cry, and she spun, immediately recognizing her son's wailing. She saw, on the far side of the square, Guwayne. He lay there all alone, crying up to the heavens.

Heart breaking, Gwen tried to run for him, but as she did, she found herself stumbling in the mud.

"Guwayne!" she cried.

Gwen ran, stumbling, until finally she reached him. She scooped him up and held him tight, crying, rocking him. She could not understand how he had gotten here, all alone.

65

Gwendolyn looked up and saw standing before her, beneath the great arched gate to the city, her father. King MacGil. He was expressionless, his face hard and cold, and he stared back, grim.

"My daughter," he boomed, his voice sounding so far away. "Leave this place. Leave it at once."

Gwen gripped Guwayne, crying and screeching in her arms; she was about to respond, to ask her father what he was doing here, what he was warning against, when suddenly she heard a flapping of wings. She craned her neck and looked up to the sky, and she finally saw a dragon swooping down from the clouds. At first she was elated, expecting it was Ralibar; but then she was horrified to see that it was not him. It was a hideous dragon, yellow in color, one she had never seen before, with long, razor-sharp teeth, a head too big for its body, and wings covered in spikes and thorns.

The dragon arched its neck, shrieking to the skies, then lowered its head and breathed fire, right for her. A wall of flame raced through the air, and Gwen screamed and clutched her baby to her chest to protect him from the heat. She flinched and ducked, yet try as she did to get away, she felt the flames slowly burning her alive.

Gwen woke screaming. She sat up in bed, breathing hard, looking everywhere, trying to brush off the flames. She jumped out of bed, and it took her a moment to realize it was just a nightmare.

Gwen stood in her castle chamber, sweating, breathing hard. Slowly, she caught her breath and looked out and saw the first of the rising suns through her window, the room spreading with violet. She looked over and saw Guwayne sleeping soundly in his crib beside her bed. She breathed deep, realizing all was well in the world.

Gwen crossed the room, splashed water on her face, then gravitated toward the arched open-air window. She looked out, bracing herself for the worst after that dream.

But all was peaceful in her kingdom. Her entire court was asleep and no one stirred. From all appearances, there was no reason to fear.

Yet as Gwen stood there, her dream hung over her like a blanket. She sensed that the visions she saw were real; she sensed it was all a warning, that she had to get out of this place—and get her people out of this place. They had to evacuate. She could not wait another moment.

Gwendolyn quickly dressed, crossed her chamber, and threw open the door.

Her guards turned and stared at her, stiffening at attention.

"My lady," one said.

She looked back at him with the gravity of a Queen. She was resolved—whatever the fallout would be.

"Sound the evacuation horns," she commanded. "Now."

There was no mistaking the authority in her voice, and her attendants looked at her, eyes widening in surprise. But they executed her command, and immediately running off and hurrying to do her will.

Gwen turned, scooped up Guwayne, and prepared to gather her most precious things. She took one long last look at this castle chamber, then went to the window and looked out at King's Court for the last time. She knew she would never see it again.

\*

Gwendolyn stood in the center of the courtyard of King's Court in the early morning sun, surrounded by thousands of her people, an agitated and angry mob. Beside her stood Steffen and Aberthol and all her counselors, along with her brothers, Godfrey and Kendrick. They stood by her side, in support of the Queen, as the mob confronted her angrily. Around the periphery of King's Court stood hundreds of her soldiers, watching warily, holding their weapons, prepared, on her nod, to take action on those people who refused to evacuate.

After the horns had sounded, her people had all gathered here in the courtyard, soldiers forcing them from their homes; now here they stood, bleary-eyed, an angry mob facing her, demanding answers. She had never seen her people so upset with her, and she did not like the feeling. This was not the experience of being Queen that she had come to know.

"We demand answers!" someone yelled from the crowd, and the huge mob cheered angrily.

"You cannot just take us all from our homes like this!" cried out another.

"Why are you demanding evacuation? We're not under attack!"

"I shall not run from my birth-given home while in the most fortified city on earth!"

"We want answers!"

The crowd cheered again. Gwendolyn faced them all, feeling hated by her people. Yet deep down, however hard it was, she knew she was doing the right thing.

Gwen stepped forward and there came a lull, as all eyes turned to her in the silence.

"I had a dream," Gwen called out to the crowd. "A dream of destruction, coming for us."

"A dream!" someone yelled.

The entire crowd laughed derisively.

"Are we to uproot and leave our whole lives behind for your dreams?"

The crowd cheered, and Gwendolyn felt her face flush, embarrassed.

"Gwendolyn is your queen, and you shall treat her respectfully!" Steffen yelled out angrily.

Gwendolyn laid a reassuring hand on his wrist; she appreciated his support, but she did not want him to incite the crowd further.

"If you wish to leave based on your dreams," one of them yelled out, "then do so! We shall find ourselves a new ruler!"

Another cheer.

"We will not leave!" another yelled.

The crowd shouted, rising to a fever pitch.

Godfrey rushed forward beside her and faced the crowd, waving his arms.

"Gwendolyn has always been a good and fair queen to you!" he yelled. "She has stood by you through thick and thin. Now you must return the favor. If she has cause to believe we should evacuate, then you must listen!"

"Even good queens can make bad decisions!" a crowd member yelled, to the cheers of others.

Gwen looked out at the faces, and she could see every one of them was angry, determined, and perhaps afraid. None of them wanted to venture out into the unknown. She could understand.

"I understand how you feel!" Gwendolyn yelled out. "But my decision is not based on dreams alone. It is based on prophecies. Ancient prophecies that I've read. Portents that I've seen coming. Argon's predictions. I do not believe King's Court will stand much longer. I want you all in safety before it happens. I know it is hard for you to leave your homes. I myself do not wish to leave my home. I love King's Court. But I ask you to trust me. I understand the unknown is hard. But it will be safer than where we are now."

"How can we trust you when you show us no danger?" one of them yelled, and the crowd cheered in agreement.

"We shall not leave     !" another yelled.

As the crowd roared and cheered, Gwendolyn could not believe what she saw before her. Were the masses so fickle? Could they really love her one moment, and hate her the next?

Gwen recalled something her father had once said to her, something she hadn't understood at the time. *The masses will love you and the masses will hate you. It is a trap to be swayed by either.*

"I'm sorry," Gwendolyn said, "but I am your leader, and I must decide what is best. If you do not leave voluntarily, my soldiers will have to forcibly escort you out of the city. This city is being gated up and evacuated—and no one will stay behind. Not on my watch."

Boos and jeers rose up, and a man stepped forward and faced Kendrick.

"This is why a woman should not rule over us," the man said. "A woman gives in to her fickle dreams. You are King MacGil's firstborn son. We would rather have *you* lead us."

The crowd cheered behind him, and Gwen could not believe what she was hearing. Kendrick reddened.

69

"This is *your* time," the man continued. "Take over the rulership of the MacGils. The Silver will answer to you. We shall not listen to her—but we shall listen to you."

Gwendolyn looked at Kendrick, dismayed, and wondered how he would react. She knew that he did not agree with evacuation. This was his chance, indeed.

A tense silence fell over the crowd until finally Kendrick spoke up.

"I stand with my sister!" he boomed. "I shall always honorably serve my Queen—whether I agree with her or not. That is what our father would want. And that is our code of honor."

The crowd, surprised and disappointed, raised their fists and jeered.

"SILVER!" Kendrick boomed. "Your Queen has spoken. Fulfill her command! Evacuate this city at once!"

A chorus of horns sounded, and the crowd jeered and shoved as thousands of Silver closed in on them, corralling them toward the gates. The crowd pushed back, fighting them. But the Silver were armed, wore armor, and were an elite fighting force, and the crowd was no match for them. The Silver pushed them slowly and steadily, all the way to the city gates.

Slowly, the city emptied, one person at a time.

Gwen stood watching it all, and she came up beside Kendrick as he watched, too.

"Thank you, my brother," she said, laying a hand on his wrist. "I shall never forget this."

He turned to her and nodded, yet his face was grave.

"I hope you know what you're doing, my sister," he said.

Gwen looked at him, feeling torn herself, as she watched her people leave this city and prepared to join them.

"I hope so too," she said.

She joined Kendrick, Godfrey, Steffen, Aberthol, and all of her advisors as they followed the masses, exiting the gates of King's Court, this time, Gwendolyn knew, for good.

# CHAPTER TWELVE

Thor writhed, trying to break free of the grip of the white snake—but it was just too strong. Its muscular body wrapped around him from his ankles to his chest, squeezing him in a vise. It now faced him, hissing, preparing to bring its open fangs down on Thor's throat.

Thor tried to buck, to thrash, to do anything—but he was helpless. All he could do was close his eyes and turn as he braced himself for the inevitable snakebite in his face.

Thor did not comprehend what was happening here, in this place. He had always imagined that when he'd found the Land of the Druids, he would be welcome, greeted by his mother. He expected that he would instantly recognize it as his home. He had expected nothing like this.

And now, Thor could not believe that he would spend his final moments here, would die here, so close to finding his mother, at the mercy of this awful beast.

As Thor braced himself, he opened his eyes, forcing himself to watch his final seconds on Earth. And as the snake lowered its fangs, suddenly Thor spotted motion out of the corner of his eye. It was a man, perhaps in his fifties, a large figure, with a long beard and shaggy brown hair—a man that Thor dimly recognized. He wore resplendent armor, the armor of a King, and he, upon seeing Thor, rushed forward, reached out with his gauntlet, and grabbed the snake by the throat, snatching it in midair, just inches before it could sink its teeth into Thor's face.

Thor watched in amazement as the man squeezed the snake by the throat, harder and harder, the snake hissing and gasping. Thor felt the snake's muscles slowly relax around his body, as the man squeezed the life out of it.

As the snake began to loosen, Thor wiggled one arm free and raised his sword and chopped its body in half.

The half of the snake wrapped around Thor fell limply to the ground, but the other half, which the man held, still struggled to live. The man squeezed it harder and harder until finally, the snake's eyes bulged open, then closed, and its body went limp in the man's hand.

As the man threw the snake's carcass down to the ground, Thor looked up at him in disbelief. It was a man he recognized; a man he'd loved; a man he'd missed dearly; a man he thought he would never see again.

King MacGil.

*

As King MacGil dropped the snake's head, he looked at Thor, smiling broadly through his beard, and stepped forward and gave him a hug, embracing him as a father would a son.

"My King," Thor said over his shoulder, as MacGil pulled back and looked at him.

"Thorgrinson," MacGil said, clasping a warm hand on Thor's shoulder, smiling down with approval. "I told you we would meet again."

Thor was speechless. He did not understand what was happening. Had he died and gone to heaven? Or was he losing his mind?

"But…how?" Thor asked. "How are you here? Are you alive?"

King MacGil smiled, put his arm around Thor, turned, and began to walk with him, leading him down a country path.

"You always had so many questions."

"Have I died?" Thor asked.

King MacGil laughed in delight, and Thor was elated to hear it. The King's laugh was a sound he had missed dearly; indeed, he hadn't realized until this day how much he had missed seeing him. In some ways, though he had known him so briefly, King MacGil was like a father to Thor, and seeing him was like having his father back.

"No, my boy," King MacGil answered, still laughing, "you have not died. In fact, you've just begun to live. You are about to truly live."

"But…you died. How are you here?"

"None of us die, really," MacGil replied. "I'm no longer in the physical plane, that is true; but I'm very much alive otherwise. In the Land of the Druids, the veil between the living and the dead is thinner, more translucent. It is easier to cross. Your mother sent me here to find you. To guide you to her."

Thor's eyes opened wide in surprise and excitement at the mention of his mother.

"So she *does* exist," Thor said.

MacGil smiled.

"Very much so." He sighed. "One cannot traverse this land without a guide. I shall be yours. You should have waited for me patiently, at the gate, to come get you. Then you wouldn't have gotten yourself into all this trouble. But you were always impatient, Thorgrinson. And that is why I love you!" he said with a laugh.

They wound their way down a path, and Thor took it all in, wondering.

"I don't understand this place at all," Thor said. "It feels so familiar…and yet, so foreign."

MacGil nodded.

"The Land of the Druids is different for each person who enters it," he said. "It is a different place for me than for you. We might even see two different lands. You see, Thorgrinson, everything you see here is merely a reflection of your own consciousness. Your own memories, your own hopes and needs and wants and fears. Your desires. You might pass through here and see your hometown; see your first love; see any place that was of importance to you; see the peak moments of your life play out before you. You might encounter your most glorious times, your highest ambitions—and you might also encounter your darkest demons. In that way, the Land of the Druids is the safest and most pleasurable place on the planet—and yet also the darkest and most dangerous. It all depends on you. On your mind. On your demons. On how you perceive yourself. How you perceive the world. And most of all, on how deeply you can control your mind.

Can you shut out a dark thought? Can you give power to a positive one?"

Thor took it all in, overwhelmed, trying to understand. He realized something as he listened to the King's words.

"You," Thor said, "you are a reflection of my mind."

MacGil nodded back, smiling.

"You loved me," he said. "I was an important person to you. A mentor of sorts."

"When I leave this place, you'll be gone," Thor said, beginning to understand, and saddened at the thought.

MacGil nodded.

"When you leave—*if* you ever leave—then yes, the world will go back to as you know it. But for now, here we are. As real and as alive as we ever were. Your entire mind, your entire consciousness, is spread out before you. Don't you see, Thorgrin," he said, draping one arm around his shoulder, "this entire land is a reflection of *you*. It is an exercise in mind control, Thorgrinson. Some of your happiest moments, some of your most beautiful memories, will appear before you on your journey. Though I must warn you: do not let your dark thoughts overwhelm you, even for an instant. Dark thoughts pass through the Land of the Druids like fierce storms. If you do not learn to control them, they will destroy you."

Thor gulped, nervous, beginning to understand.

"So that town I past," Thor realized, "my hometown. I created that. My mind created that."

MacGil nodded.

"It was an important place in your life. It was the place you wanted to welcome you."

Thor realized something else.

"And then that field of flowers I walked through," he said, "it was indeed where I first dated Gwendolyn. And that white snake I saw…"

Thor trailed off, piecing it all together. It was beginning to make sense. Finally, he was understanding. This place was more powerful than he'd realized. More amazing, more promising, than he'd ever dreamed. And yet also more terrifying.

They walked for a long while in silence, until something occurred to Thor.

"And my mother?" he asked. "Is she alive? Is she a real person? Or just a figment of my hope and imagination? Is she here only because she exists somewhere deep in my subconscious? Only because I always wanted her to exist? Only because I needed her to exist? Only because I dreamed of having a glorious parent?"

King MacGil was silent, expressionless, as they walked.

"You seek absolute answers," he said. "In the Land of the Druids, you will find there are no absolutes. The only answers you'll find are within yourself. However powerful you are inside, that is how powerful this world will be before you. Prepare yourself, young Thorgrin, and steel yourself to control the hardest, greatest, most unwieldy weapon of all: your mind."

*

Thor traversed the Land of the Druids for hours, MacGil by his side. The two of them had been laughing and bantering for hours, reminiscing about the old times, about the hunts they had taken together, about King's Court, about when Thor had first met the King's daughter. They talked about MacGil's accepting him into his family; they talked about battle, and knights, and honor, and valor. They talked about King MacGil's assassin, and the vengeance that had been taken. They talked of politics. But mostly they talked of battle. They were both fearless warriors at their heart, and they understood each other on a deep level. In some ways, Thor felt as if he were here talking to himself. It felt so good to be talking to King MacGil again, to have him back at his side. Thor felt a sense of a break from reality, as if he were wandering in a surreal land, in a dream from which there was no waking up.

They passed through vistas that Thor recognized with delight, places that felt so familiar, places from his hometown, from his countryside, from outside King's Court. He felt so comfortable here. A part of him could dimly feel his mind creating these places as he went, and it was hard to separate the two; Thor felt as if he were standing at a strange intersection between his own mind and the external reality of the world. It was scary to him to realize the depth of power of his mind. If he could create anything, that meant he could create the most glorious kingdoms with the snap of a finger. Yet if he had a moment of weakness, that meant that, in just a few moments, he could create the darkest kingdoms. That terrified him. How could he keep his mind filled with positive thoughts all the time?

They crested a hill and both stopped, looking out. Thor gasped, awestruck at the sight. He could hardly fathom it: spread out below was King's Court. It was a perfect replica, so real that Thor was certain it was the real thing. It looked more glorious than he had ever seen it, thousands of knights in shining armor standing before the ancient stone walls, standing before the portcullis, lining the parapets. There were more knights than he'd ever seen, glorious warriors protecting a glorious city.

King MacGil stood beside him and smiled.

"Your mind is a beautiful place, Thorgrin," he said, looking out and admiring the view. "I never had that many knights in King's Court. It seems you have increased their ranks!"

King MacGil threw back his head and laughed.

"In fact, I don't think I have ever seen that many knights at once," he added. "The shining of their armor blinds me. You truly are a warrior at heart."

Thor had a hard time believing his mind was creating this; it all seemed so real, so perfect, more real than anything he'd ever seen.

Thor set out on the path with MacGil, the road perfectly immaculate, heading toward the gates. As they went, thousands more knights appeared on the road and stiffened at attention, lined all up and down the road. Trumpets sounded in the distance.

They crossed the bridge, over the moat, under the portcullis, and into King's Court. As they passed beneath the massive, arched stone

76

gates, waiting to greet them was a single person, smiling, hand outstretched to them.

Gwendolyn.

Thor beamed at the sight of her. She looked more beautiful than ever, with her long blonde hair, bright blue eyes, wearing a regal dress, smiling and holding one hand out for Thor.

Thor hurried to her and embraced her and she leaned in and kissed him, hugging him tight.

Then they turned and walked through King's Court together, King MacGil falling in beside his daughter.

"I'm glad that you envision my daughter in such a beautiful light," King MacGil whispered to him. "I see her the same way."

"Thorgrinson," Gwendolyn whispered, clasping one hand around his arm, leaning in and kissing his cheek. He could feel her love for him, and it revived him.

"Gwendolyn," he said, clasping her hand, holding it tight. Suddenly, Thor remembered. "Where's Guwayne?"

No sooner had he spoken the words then there came the cry of a baby. Thor looked over to see his son in Gwendolyn's arms. She held him gently, cradling him, smiling.

Thor reached out and took the boy, who leapt into his arms, bigger and older than Thor remembered. Guwayne hugged Thor, and Thor hugged him back.

"Daddy," Guwayne said into his ear.

It was the first time Thor had ever heard him speak. It was surreal.

Suddenly, Gwendolyn and MacGil stopped, and Thor turned to see why. As he saw, he stopped, too.

Standing before them was a man who meant more to Thor than just about anyone: Argon. He stood dressed in his white cloak and hood, holding his staff, his eyes shining as he stared back, expressionless.

"Thorgrinson," Argon said.

Thor reached out and handed Guwayne back to Gwen, but as he looked down, he saw that Guwayne was gone. Vanished.

Thor looked over at Gwendolyn, but saw that she was gone, too. So was King MacGil. In fact, as he spun, he saw that everyone—all the knights, all the people that had filled King's Court just moments before—had disappeared.

The city now stood empty. Now it was just Thor and Argon, standing in this empty place, facing each other.

"It is time to further your training," Argon said. "Only here, in the Land of the Druids, can you begin to reach the highest levels of who you are; can you begin to tap the deepest levels of your powers. Only here can you understand what it means to be who you are, what it means to be a Druid."

Thor fell in beside Argon as the two of them walked through King's Court. There was nothing but silence, and the howling of the wind. Finally, Thor spoke.

"What does it mean to be a Druid?" Thor asked.

"It means to be everything and nothing. To be a Druid, one must master nature, and one must master one's self. It means to combine the frailty of being human with the limitless power of harnessing nature. Do you see that lion, there, charging us?"

Thor turned and saw a fierce lion racing for them. His heart raced with fear as it neared, yet Argon simply held out a hand, and the lion stopped as it leapt and fell to their feet, harmless.

Argon lowered his palm.

"The lion opposes you, until you understand its nature. There is a current that underlies all things. Here in the Land of the Druids, the current is not beneath the surface. The current *is* the surface."

"I feel it," Thor said, closing his eyes, breathing in deeply, holding up his palms to the wind. "I sense it. It is like…a thickness to the air…the slightest of vibrations, like something humming in the sky."

Argon nodded in approval.

"Yes. It is like running your palm over rushing water. It is everywhere, and here, it is easier for you to harness it, to understand it. And yet it is also easier for you to lose control."

Thor turned and saw a bear charging for him, roaring, at full speed. Thor's first impulse was to turn and run, but instead he held out his palm, feeling the energy of this place, knowing that it was only nature. Only energy. Energy that he could harness.

Thor held out both palms, waiting, despite his fear, forcing himself to stay calm; at the last second, the bear leapt, roaring, then stopped. It stood there, its paws in the air, flailing, and finally, it lowered itself down to the ground and rolled onto its back.

Argon turned and walked away, and Thor, amazed, turned and hurried to catch up.

The two walked and walked, leaving the gates of King's Court, Thor wondering where they were going.

"If you hope to meet your mother," Argon said, finally, "you have a far journey ahead of you. The Land of the Druids is not a land that you cross at your leisure. It is a land that you must *earn* to cross. It must admit you. It is a land that demands of you, that tests you. Only the worthy can cross it. Your mother is at the farthest end of this land. It will take everything you have to reach her. You must become stronger."

"But how?" Thor asked.

"You will have to learn to purge yourself of the demons that lurk within you. Of old, painful memories. Of anyone who mistreated you. Of feelings of anger, hate, vengeance. Of hurt and pain. You must learn to rise above them, to leave them in the past. It is the ultimate test of a warrior—and of a Druid."

Thor furrowed his brow as they walked, trying to understand.

"But how do I do that?" he asked.

Argon stopped, and Thor looked out and saw stretched before them an endless landscape of gloom. The land was mud, punctuated by dead trees, and the dark clouds that glowered above it matched its color. A slow-winding river cutting its way through it, its water the color of mud, and Thor realized at once where he was.

"The Underworld," Thorgrin said, remembering the Empire. "The Land of the Dead."

Argon nodded.

"A place of your darkest dreams," he said. "An endless and vast wasteland. It lies inside you. The darkness, along with the light. And you must cross this. It is the first step in the journey."

Thor gazed out with dread at the barren land, hearing the awful sound of distant crows, feeling the intense gloom pervading this place. He turned to Argon to ask him more—but was surprised to see him already gone.

Thor turned back to look for the safety of King's Court, wondering if he should turn around—but it was gone now, too. He stood alone, in the center of this endless wasteland, surrounded by death, by the darkest corners of his psyche—and with no way out but through.

# CHAPTER THIRTEEN

Reece ran through the driving rain with Stara, Matus, and Srog by his side, stumbling their way down the muddy slope in the black of night. Matus ran with one arm clamped around the waist of Srog, who was limping badly, while Reece clutched Stara's hand, not out of love, but to keep her from slipping, and to keep himself from slipping too. He felt guilty even touching it, thinking of Selese, but given the situation, he had no choice.

They all ran along the edge of the cliff, slipping in the mud as they went, careful not to fall over the edge. Reece knew the sea was not far, the crashing waves somewhere below, and yet he was barely able to hear them over the sound of the pounding rain. With the number of soldiers awaiting them out there, Reece knew they were likely on a suicide mission. He knew that the Upper Islanders would be waiting for them in force at the shores, blocking any possible escape route for them, any dream of making it to his sister's fleet, which was harbored out at sea.

Reece no longer cared. At least they had a plan and would die with honor, not sitting as cowards in that cave. A part of him, anyway, had died with Selese, and now he just fought for survival.

Reece knew they hadn't much time before daybreak, when the Upper Islanders would surely move to take vengeance on his sister's fleet. Even if they didn't make the safety of the ship, Reece knew they had to at least try to reach the fleet to warn them. Reece could not allow them all to die, could not allow their deaths to be on his head. After all, he was the one who had killed Tirus and who had unwittingly set them all up for retribution.

The cliffs finally gave way to a steep mountain slope, and they stumbled downward, trying to make for the shore below, slipping and propping each other up. Reece saw the ocean spread out below, and finally was close enough to hear their crashing waves over the sound of the rain.

They reached a small plateau and they all paused, breathing hard.

"Leave me," Srog said, gasping, clutching his side. "My wound cannot sustain this."

"No one gets left behind," Reece insisted.

Reece gasped for air as he looked down and saw hundreds of Tirus's men fanned out on the shores, standing guard, on the lookout, blocking their escape to the ships—and also blocking the ships from reaching shore. Reece knew the only reason they hadn't been killed yet was because of the cover of darkness, and because of the blinding wind and rain and fog.

"There," Stara said, pointing.

Reece followed her finger and saw dozens more of Tirus's men pressed inside a cave on the shore, sheltered from the wind. They were dunking long arrows into buckets, then wrapping the tips of the arrows in cloth, slowly, meticulously, again and again.

"Oil," Stara said. "They're preparing to set their arrows aflame. Those arrows are long. They're meant for the ships. They intend to set the fleet aflame."

Reece watched, horrified, and realized she was right. He felt a pit in his stomach as he realized how close Gwendolyn's ships were to being lost.

"Those arrows would never fly in this wind and rain," Matus said.

"They don't need to," Stara countered. "As soon as the rain stops, they will."

"We haven't much time," Srog said. "How do you propose we fight our way through all those men? How can we reach the Queen's ships?"

Reece scanned the shores. He looked out at the ships, bobbing in the rough waters, anchored perhaps a hundred yards offshore; the sailors surely had no idea what had happened on shore, no idea of what was about to happen to them. He could not let them get hurt. And he also needed to reach them for their own escape. Reece surveyed the landscape, wondering how they could do it.

82

"We can swim," Reece said.

Srog shook his head.

"I'd never make it," he replied.

"None of us would," Matus added. "Those waters are rougher than they look. You are not from here; you do not understand. The tides are fierce in the open sea. We would all drown. I'd rather die on dry land than at sea."

"What about those rocks?" Stara suddenly said.

They all turned and followed her finger. As he peered into the rain, wiping water from his eyes, Reece saw a jetty of rocks, jutting out into the ocean perhaps thirty yards.

"If we can make it to the edge of those rocks, my arrows can reach," Stara said, lifting her bow.

"Can reach what?" Matus asked.

"The closest ship," she said, as if it were the most obvious thing in the world.

Reece looked at her, confused.

"And why would you fire on our own ships?"

Stara shook her head, impatient.

"You don't understand," she said. "We can attach a rope to the arrow. If the arrow lodges in the deck, it will give us a line. It can guide us through the waters. We can pull ourselves as we swim to the ship."

Reece looked at her, impressed by her bold plan. The idea was crazy enough that it just might work.

"And what are the Queen's men going to do when they see an arrow with a rope lodging into their ship in the black of night?" Srog asked. "They will cut it off. Or they will kill us. How should they know it is us?"

Reece thought quickly.

"The MacGil sign," he said. "The falcon's claws. Any MacGil of the Ring will recognize it. Three arrows shot straight into the sky, all of them aflame. If we shoot them off first, they'll know it's us, not the enemy."

Srog looked at Reece skeptically.

"And how are you going to get flaming arrows to last in weather like this?"

"They don't need to last," Reece replied. "They just need to stay aflight for a few seconds, just long enough for the sailors to see them, before the rains will put them out."

Srog shook his head.

"It all sounds like craziness to me," he said.

"Do you have any better ideas?" Reece asked.

Srog shook his head.

"Then it's settled," Reece said.

"That rope there," said Stara, pointing. "The long one, coiled up, on the beach, near Tirus's men. It is just long enough. That's what we need. We can tie it to the arrow and make it work."

"And if your brother's men spot us?" Srog asked.

Stara shrugged.

"Then we shall be killed by our own men."

"And what of those ten men there, blocking the entrance to the jetty?" Srog asked.

Reece looked out and saw six soldiers standing before it. He turned, snatched Stara's bow, grabbed an arrow, raised it high, and fired.

The arrow sailed through the air, sailing down forty yards, and pierced one of the soldiers through the throat. He dropped dead.

"I count nine," Reece said, then took off at a sprint.

*

The others followed Reece as he sprinted down the hill, slipping and sliding, scrambling for the jetty. It took Tirus's men a few moments to realize that one of their own had fallen; yet soon enough they did, and they all drew their weapons, on guard, peering out into the night for the enemy.

Reece and the others raced recklessly for the chokepoint leading out to the jetty, Reece feeling that if they got their fast enough, just maybe they could kill the soldiers guarding it before they knew what hit them. More importantly, maybe they could get past them.

"Attack them, but no matter what, don't stop running!" Reece yelled to the others. "We're not here to fight them all—we just need to make it past them, to the end of the jetty."

The blackness of early morning was beginning to lift as they all ran, swords drawn, Reece gasping for air as his feet hit the sand, stumbling, realizing this might be the last run of his life. The group of soldiers blocking the jetty did not see them either, their attention on their soldier who had fallen, all of them baffled as to who had killed him. Three of the soldiers sat hunched over him, trying to revive him.

That was their fatal mistake. Reece and Matus lunged forward as they reached them, Srog hobbling just behind them, swords drawn, and before the three soldiers, their sides exposed, realized, they stabbed each one through the heart. That left six of them.

Stara, right behind them, drew her dagger and backhanded one, slicing his throat, dropping him to the ground; then she turned seamlessly and stabbed another through the heart. That left four.

Reece backhanded one with his gauntlet and kicked another, while Srog head-butted one and Matus ducked as an attacker swung a mace for his head, then rose up and sliced his stomach.

Within moments the group of soldiers blocking the jetty was down, as Reece and the others blew past them like a storm.

A horn sounded, and Reece turned to see that Tirus's other men—hundreds of them—had spotted them. There rose a great battle cry on the beach, as the men turned and began racing for them.

"The rope!" Stara shouted.

Reece ran over to the huge coil of rope nearby and hoisted it over his shoulder; it was heavier than he'd imagined. Matus rushed over and helped him, and they hoisted it together as they all ran down the jetty, the four of them running as fast as they could. Stara brought up the rear, and she stopped, turned, raised her bow, and fired six shots in procession, taking out six of the closest soldiers, the bodies piling up at the base the jetty.

They all, gasping for air, finally reached the edge of the jetty. Waves crashed all around them, foam spraying up over their feet. Reece lost his footing for a moment, and Stara reached out and steadied him. Beside them, Srog and Matus hurried to tie the rope to the end of one of Stara's arrows.

"The warning sign first!" Reece called out, reminding Stara.

Stara took three arrows from a closed quiver wrapped around her back. These were wrapped with an oil-soaked cloth, prepared in advance, as all good archers did, in their own separate quiver. Out of the quiver she also removed the dry flint rocks and struck them together, creating sparks. She did it again and again, the sparks not catching in the rain. Reece turned to see Tirus's men storming the jetty. He knew their time was short.

"Come on!" Reece cried.

Finally, the cloth sparked, and all three arrows lit up.

"Shoot them up high!" Reece said. "Nearly straight overhead! But angle a little toward the ships! That is the sign!"

Stara fired the three flaming arrows in quick succession, and they shot up, close to each other, perfect shots. It was the flame of the falcon's claws, high up in the sky, the ancient sign of the MacGils, and any good commander watching the skies would see. Reece was relieved to see that the arrows stayed aflame for a good five seconds, until finally, all three fizzled out.

"The rope!" Matus said. "Fire it now!"

Stara took up the rope and arrow, aiming high, long distance for the ship.

"We've got one shot at this," Reece said to her. "Do not miss."

She turned and looked at him, and he was struck by how beautiful her face was in the rain, how proud, how noble—how fearless. He stared back at her and nodded reassuringly.

"You can do this," he said. "I have faith in you."

She nodded back.

Stara turned and fired, and they all watched, Reece holding his breath, as the arrow sailed up high, arching through the air. Reece knew that if it fell short, they would all be finished.

Finally, in the distance, Reece heard the satisfying thunk of arrow piercing wood, and as Reece saw the rope stiffen below, he knew she had hit: the arrow was lodged in the ship. The rope uncoiled as it sailed through the air, and there were but a few feet of it left as it finally lodged into its resting place.

Reece turned and saw hundreds of Tirus's men shouting, too close now, drawing their swords and bows and closing in on them.

"The water's not getting any warmer!" Matus cried out, looking down at the churning sea.

As one, the four them of them grabbed hold of the rope and jumped off the rocks and into the foaming sea.

Reece was shocked at how cold the water was; he struggled to catch his breath as he swallowed a mouthful of salty seawater, bobbing up and down in the raging ocean. He held onto the rope, not letting go no matter what, and he pulled himself up, one foot at a time, heading toward the distant boat.

Reece pulled hard and fast, along with the others, and they all began to move their way through the water, with each pull getting farther from shore and closer to the ship.

Reece heard the muted shouts of Tirus's men on the shore behind them, and then he heard another noise which disturbed him—the noise of an arrow piercing water. The noise came again, and again, and Reece looked over to see arrows sailing through the air, piercing the water on either sides of him. He realized that Tirus's men were firing on them.

Reece heard a scream in his ear. Stara. He looked over and saw her leg pierced by an arrow, the arrow protruding from her thigh. He looked back and saw a host of arrows airborne, whizzing by their head.

Srog cried out next, and Reece saw that he, too, was pierced by an arrow.

Reece knew he had to do something fast. He reached out and grabbed Stara, draping one arm around her as she flailed.

"Hang on to me tight," he said.

He positioned his body over hers so that he was between her and the shore, putting himself in the path of the fire. Then, as she hung on, he pulled the rope for them both.

Reece shrieked as he suddenly felt an arrow pierce the side of his thigh. The pain was excruciating. But at least he took comfort in knowing that had he not been in its path, it would have hit Stara.

More and more arrows sailed by their heads, and Reece wondered how much longer they could keep this up, how much longer it would be until one of the arrows was fatal. He pulled for dear life, doubling his speed. Reece knew their situation was desperate; if they didn't have help soon, they would all be dead.

Reece heard another noise, that of an arrow sailing over his head—but this time, from another direction. He looked up in surprise to see arrows flying overhead toward shore, launching from the Queen's ship. At first Reece braced himself, thinking the Queen's men were firing upon him. But then, as he saw more and more of them fly overhead, and as he heard the cries of Tirus's men, he realized: the Queen's men were coming to their aid.

Hundreds of arrows suddenly flew overhead from the Queen's ship, killing Tirus's men firing at them. Soon, the arrows from the shore stopped landing beside them.

Out of danger's path, they pulled harder and harder in the churning sea—and soon, Reece felt a tug, and realized he was being pulled in by the Queen's men. Dozens of sailors grabbed the ropes and yanked hard, and soon they were being pulled, faster and faster, right for the ship.

Bobbing desperately in the waves, gasping for air, all of them, wounded, reached the edge of the ship. A hand reached down for Reece, and as he grabbed it he looked up and saw one of his own, a MacGil from the mainland, eager to help.

The sailor looked down and smiled.

"Good to have you on board," he said.

## CHAPTER FOURTEEN

Romulus led the way, marching before his million-man army as they crested the final hill on the approach to King's Court. As his horse reached the top, Luanda bound behind him, the vista opened up before him, and his heart soared with anticipation.

But Romulus was puzzled by what he saw. He had expected to see the city packed with people, had expected to catch his nemesis, Gwendolyn, unaware. He had expected to see all of her men, the Silver, the last bastion of strength of the Ring, conveniently assembled in one place for him to wipe out with his dragons. He had been looking forward to this moment, reliving it in his head, preparing to revel in this peak moment of his victory.

But Romulus was dumbfounded at what he saw before him. From here, he could see through the gates, into King's Court, and he could not reconcile the image: it was empty.

Gwendolyn had fled. Somehow, she had known he was coming, he did not know how. She had outsmarted him once again.

"It cannot be," Romulus said out loud, not understanding. Where could she have gone? How could she have known he was coming? Romulus had been meticulous about destroying everyone in his path—there was no way a messenger could have reached her. He had even made a point of keeping back his dragons, so that they would not hear their cries, not see the devastation they had wrought.

Yet despite all of his preparations, all of his careful planning, somehow Gwendolyn had found out. How could she have evacuated this entire city so quickly?

His face flushed in rage. She had robbed him of his victory.

And most confusing of all: where could they have gone? The Ring was a finite space, he knew, and there was only so far they could go to hide.

Romulus, enraged, kicked his horse with a cry, and charged down the well-maintained road, right for the wide-open gates of King's Court—left open as if to tantalize him. All of his men joined him, racing behind him, Luanda still bound behind him on his horse, as they rode right into the great city.

Romulus could barely contain his rage; his greatest moment of satisfaction had been stripped from him. He had been dreaming of destroying these gates himself, of murdering everyone in his path, of setting fire to the place and enjoying the screams of pain.

Now there was nothing for him to do but walk inside.

It did not feel like a victory at all. It felt like a defeat. Half the fun of taking a city was inflicting pain, torture, devastation. No, this was not a victory at all.

Romulus's men cheered as they rode into the city, and the sound of their cries inflamed him even more; stupid idiots, celebrating a victory that they didn't even achieve. Romulus could not stand it anymore.

Romulus jumped down from his horse, yanking Luanda down with him, stormed up to the first soldier he found, drew his sword, and chopped off his head. He then charged forward and chopped off another head; then another; then another.

Finally, his soldiers got the point. They all stopped their revelry and grew quiet as they made way for him. They lined up at attention, awaiting his command, trembling in fear. The courtyard of the city, just moments before so filled with glee, now had a pallor of death.

Romulus stood in the center of his men as they cleared a circle around him, and boomed out:

"There is no victory to celebrate, fools! On the contrary, you should be ashamed. You have all been outsmarted by a *girl* queen. She has evaded us, has rescued her people from our grasp. Is this cause to celebrate?"

His men stood still, not moving a muscle, as Romulus strode up and down the ranks, debating whether to kill some more of them. He had to vent his rage somehow. Not one of them stirred; they knew him too well.

Romulus, hands on his hips, turned and scanned the walls, scanned everywhere, hoping for a sign of somebody, of any life at all. But there was none. Where could they have gone?

A shrill cry pierced the air, followed by a flapping of wings; it grew louder, and soon over Romulus's head there appeared his host of dragons. They circled furiously, they too enraged, their great talons hanging below them as they swooped down, then up, circling again and again, as if wanting to breathe fire on them all. Romulus could feel their rage at the lack of bloodshed. It was a rage he shared.

What sort of a victory would this be without death and destruction? What sort of a victory would it be without knowing that Gwendolyn was dead, crushed beneath his feet, and that all of her people were annihilated?

As Romulus wondered where Gwendolyn could be, suddenly he had an idea. Who else would know where that crafty girl would have gone, except one of her own?

Romulus looked over at Luanda; she stood several feet away, gagged, squirming against her ropes, her wrists and ankles still bound behind her back. Romulus rushed forward, raised his knife, and her eyes opened wide with fear as he came close.

But he reached out and sliced her binds, including her gag.

"Where is your sister?" Romulus demanded.

Luanda, free from her binds, rubbing her wrists, glared back.

"How should I know?" she said. "You've got me tied up like an animal. You filthy pig."

Luanda reached back and smacked her palm across his face, a smack that echoed in front of all of his men. Romulus's first impulse was to punch her back, and to hit her harder than she hit him. But he restrained himself. The smack actually felt good, shook him from his dark thoughts, and he admired her fiery spirit, the way she looked back at him with such venom. It actually made him smile: he loved seeing someone as filled with rage as himself.

"Tell me where she is," he repeated slowly. "You know her. You know this place. Why did she leave? Where did she go?"

Luanda put her hands on her hips, looking all about King's Court, as if debating.

"And if I did know," she said, "why would I tell you?"

Romulus stared at her, his expression darkening. But he knew he needed her, and forced himself to use his most seductive voice.

He took a step closer to her and smiled, raising one hand and stroking her hair.

"Because I will make you my queen," he said softly, his voice guttural. "You will be the most powerful woman in the Empire."

He had expected her to gush in awe and gratitude; and yet instead, she surprised him: she scoffed.

"There is nothing I would rather less," she spat. "I'd rather die first."

He scowled.

"Then I will give you death," he said. "Or whatever it is you want. If you do not wish to be my queen, then just tell me what you want—anything—and you shall have it."

Luanda looked long and hard at him, as if summing him up, as if thinking. Finally, her eyes narrowed.

"What I want," she said slowly, "is to be the one to kill my sister. I want her captured alive. I want her brought to me—to me personally—to beg for mercy."

Romulus looked her up and down, shocked at her response. She was more like him than he'd thought. For the first time, he admired her.

Romulus smiled broadly. Maybe after all, he would indeed make her his queen—whether she liked it or not.

"Agreed," he said.

Luanda took several steps forward, her back to him, and scanned the gates, the courtyard, the dusty ground, seeming to think it all over.

"If I know my sister," she said, "she's planned an escape route. She always plans ahead. She plans for everything. And she's way too smart for you. If she wanted to save her people, she would not just plan to go elsewhere in the Ring—she would assume that eventually you would find her. So wherever it is she went, it would be outside the

Ring. Across the Canyon. Probably across a sea. Likely her ships are setting sail right now."

Romulus's mind spun as he pondered her words. As she spoke them, instantly, he knew that she was right. Gwendolyn *would* do something like that. She wouldn't just evacuate her people only to be found inside the Ring. How stupid he had been.

He looked at Luanda with a whole new respect. And he realized, if he was to stop Gwendolyn, there was little time left.

Romulus leaned back, craned his neck up to the heavens, and raised his palms.

"DRAGONS!" he shrieked. "TO THE CANYON!"

The dragons screeched in unison as Romulus commanded them. His men could not reach the Canyon crossing in time to stop her, or the sea—but his dragons could. They could fly out in front for him, a flying army, and eviscerate Gwendolyn before he reached her.

It would rob him of some satisfaction.

But it was better than none at all.

## CHAPTER FIFTEEN

Erec opened his eyes as the gentle rocking motion shook him from his sleep. He looked about, disoriented, trying to figure out where he was. In all his years as a warrior, he had never allowed himself to fall asleep, especially in a strange environment. It was a profoundly disorienting feeling for him to now awake and have no sense at all of where he was.

Erec blinked and realized he was lying on his back in a small boat, perhaps twenty feet long, a crude canvas sail attached to a mast. The boat rocked gently in the huge, rolling ocean waves, lifting them up and down, as if lulling them to sleep.

Erec looked up at the sky above them, in awe at its beauty. He looked up and saw open sky as far as the eye could see, the entire world coming alive in the sunrise, one vast stretch of violet and pink and purple. A warm breeze stirred, and Erec breathed deep, comforted by the ocean air, and by the soft colors of the universe. It was the most peaceful scene he'd ever encountered, and Erec realized why he'd fallen asleep.

Erec looked down at the figure lying in his arms, and realized there was an even greater reason for his sense of peace: Alistair. Erec felt her body before he saw her, and he looked at her long blonde hair, spilling down to her waist, her beautiful profile, her perfectly sculpted face, her eyes closed as she slept gently, like an angel, on his chest. Lying on his back, with Alistair in his arms and the universe spread out before him, Erec had never felt more at ease. It was as if the entire universe had been created just for the two of them.

Erec thought back and remembered the events of the night before, and his heart pounded as he recalled his capture at the hands of those mercenaries, and Alistair's nearly being attacked. He felt overwhelmed with guilt for being surprised like that, for not being able to defend her. He remembered Alistair's powers, her summoning

94

the storm, that monster, and his thoughts switched from fear to wonder. He gazed upon her angelic face, feeling the intense energy radiating off of her, and he knew she was not entirely of this earth. She was other-worldly. He wondered at the depth of the powers that coursed through her. He knew they were immense. Yet also, perhaps, unpredictable.

Though Erec was in awe of her, he was also perhaps, he had to admit, slightly afraid for her. What would her powers mean for their relationship? For their life together? For their children yet to come? Erec thought of how powerful Thorgrin was. Would Erec's sons then be equally as powerful? His daughters? And would Alistair be able to love and respect him, even though he did not have the same powers as she?

And the most troubling thought of all: what if her powers somehow led to her demise? Did she have a shorter time to live?

Erec studied her face, and he felt overwhelmed with love for her, and gratitude toward her, and he prayed that she would live forever. He was looking forward to showing her off to his people, to their wedding to come. His joy at being with her, and his excitement to introduce her to his family, overshadowed even his grief for his father's pending death.

Erec gently loosened Alistair from his chest, eager to see where they were. He rose to his knees, the boat rocking, then to his feet, balancing himself so as not to fall. He stood in the center of the boat and peered into the horizon. As he did, his heart swelled with excitement.

The Southern Isles lay just ahead, as beautiful and resplendent as Erec remembered them to be as a boy, the jagged cliffs encircling the islands rising up from the ocean like a work of art, covered in a slight mist, yellowish in color. The sun shone down directly on the isles, so strong that the islands were known as the sunny islands. They seemed as if they were glowing in the midst of the dark ocean, like giant orbs of light in the midst of darkness.

Erec sensed motion beside him, felt the boat sway slightly, and he turned to see Alistair standing beside him, smiling. She reached out and took his hand, and the two of them looked out at the islands together.

"One day you will be queen there," he said. "We shall rule the islands together."

"As long as we're together," Alistair replied, "I would go with you to the ends of the earth."

Erec's heart leapt with anticipation as each wave brought them closer and closer to the islands. Would his family be there to greet him? What would they think of Alistair? What would it be like to return to this place he had not seen since childhood?

As they came closer and closer, he wondered: would it be the same place that he had once known and loved?

*

Erec scanned the shoreline with joy as their boat touched the sand, hundreds of Southern Islanders awaiting them, cheering their arrival. His people had showed up with great fanfare, stretched out as far as the eye could see, greeting them like a king and queen. Dozens of them rushed forward and grabbed the edge of their boat and dragged it up onto the sand, as Erec jumped down and held out a hand for Alistair. She took it and stepped onto the sand.

There came a great cheer as she did, and Erec looked out, overwhelmed with pride to be so happily embraced by his people, and to be by Alistair's side. One person after the next pressed forward to embrace him, and to kiss Alistair's hand, as Erec scanned the faces, trying to recognize anyone from his childhood. It was all a blur.

Erec had forgotten how warm and friendly the Southern Islanders were, these people who were legendary for their warmth and hospitality, who, legend had it, were lit alive by the sun. They were quick to laugh and smile and give you a hug or a pat on the back; yet their kindness was never mistaken for weakness, as they were also known to be legendary warriors, an island of strong and proud and noble warriors, among the most skilled of all the countries. They were Erec's people.

As Erec embraced them back, tears flowed from his face, and he realized how much he had been missing his homeland, his people, this place where he had spent his formative years, this place he still dreamt of often. It felt so good to be home again, his feet to be back on his soil, and it felt so good to be so loved. He had not been sure if his people would even remember him, and here he was, welcomed like a returning hero.

It also warmed Erec's heart with joy to see them welcome Alistair so fondly, to treat her as if she were already one of their own, already their queen. They showered on her the same love and affection they reserved for Erec, and Erec felt eternally grateful to them for it.

During all those years Erec had spent in the Ring, ever since that day his father had shipped him off as a boy to study under the tutelage of King MacGil and his Silver, the Ring had felt like home to Erec. King MacGil had become like a father to him, and the Silver had all become his brothers. Erec had never consciously thought much of the Southern Isles, because in his mind, he had not imagined himself ever returning. In his mind, the Ring had become his home.

And yet now that he had returned, Erec felt a rush of sensations coming back to him, memories, feelings, and he realized that this place was his home, too. His first home. A place to which he owed as much loyalty as to the Ring. After all, these were his people, his blood. He had been born here, grown up here, before being shipped off to the Ring to become a great warrior.

He had achieved what his father had set out for him to achieve—had become the greatest warrior of them all—and he had done his people proud. Now, he realized, he owed his father—and his people—a debt. It was time to serve them. Duty had called, and it was time not just to see his dying father, but also to embrace the role he had been destined for since his birth: to assume the Kingship of the Southern Isles. He knew that's what his people would demand, what his father would demand, whether he liked it or not, and he was prepared to serve. With Alistair by his side as Queen, he could think of no more fitting return.

"My brother," came a voice.

Erec turned, thrilled to hear the familiar voice, and was happily surprised to see standing before him his younger brother, Strom, grinning wide.

"I would have expected your return in a more glorious ship than this!" Strom added with a laugh, as he stepped forward and embraced him.

Erec hugged him, then pulled him back and looked him up and down: he was shocked to see his younger brother, now, so many years later, a full-grown man, nearly as big as he, rippling with muscles. He had the countenance of a hardened warrior, one who had been tested by battle. He was now a man.

"Strom," Erec said, eyes glistening with approval. It felt so good to see him again.

Strom, too, looked Erec up and down, sizing him up. He shook his head.

"I was sure I'd grown enough to be taller than you! Son of a bitch! I only needed one more inch!" Strom laughed, squeezing Erec's shoulder. "But it seems I'm bigger than you at least."

Erec shook his head. That was his brother.

"You haven't changed one bit," he said. "Still trying to outdo me."

"What do you mean trying?" Strom said. "*Succeeding.* I shall show you later when we spar!"

Strom laughed heartily, and Erec knew that his little brother meant it. Erec laughed too, amazed at how quickly they picked up where they'd left off.

Erec loved his younger brother, and he'd never felt any competition or jealousy with him whatsoever. Yet Strom did not share the same point of view. For his little brother, Erec was always the man to beat, the target to outdo; Erec could swear that Strom had devoted his life to one-upping him any way he could.

Erec laughed it off, but for Strom it was a deadly serious business. Erec had met many people in his life, and yet he had never encountered a more intense sibling rivalry, even if it was one-way. His relationship with Strom had always been a mixed bag. Erec sensed

98

that Strom loved him—and yet at the same time, could not control his desire to defeat him. Erec blamed it on the competitive way his father had raised them, always pitting them against each other. His father had thought that would make them better men—but it had only created divisiveness. Erec himself did not believe in fostering competition, and if he had sons he resolved to never raise them that way; instead, Erec believed it was better to raise them to look out for each other, to watch each other's backs, and to foster loyalty and selflessness. Those, Erec believed were the true traits of a warrior. Competition was important, but not among family—competition could be learned on the field of battle, and skills could be sharpened other ways. Sometimes competition brought out the best in people, it was true—and yet other times, competition only fostered the worst.

"And bringing a bride with you?" Strom remarked, looking over Alistair, shaking his head. "Did you have to outdo me in this, too? I haven't found my bride yet, and now I doubt I shall find one as beautiful as she," Strom said, as he stepped up and took Alistair's hand and kissed it.

Alistair smiled back.

"A pleasure to meet you," she replied. "A brother to Erec is a brother to me."

"Well, you should know, before you marry him," Strom said, "that I am Erec's better brother. Spend some time here, and you might decide to choose me. After all, why would you want the weaker stock?"

Strom laughed, and Erec shook his head. Strom was as opinionated and tactless as ever.

"I know I shall find myself quite content with my current choice, thank you," Alistair replied with a smile, diplomatic as always.

Strom stepped aside as the crowd parted ways and someone stepped forward, and Erec was amazed to see who it was:

Dauphine. His younger sister.

The last time he had seen her, she had been up to his waist, and now, Erec could hardly believe how tall she had grown; she was nearly as tall as he, with broad shoulders, a perfect posture, and a dazzling smile. He could not believe how beautiful she had become, either, with her long strawberry hair and bright green eyes.

She stood there and stared back at Erec with the same intensity he remembered from when they were children. Just a few years younger, she'd always looked up to Erec as a hero, had always been intent on demanding his attention, and had always been incredibly jealous and territorial of anyone who took his attention away from her. Possibly because their father had always been absent, ruling his kingdom, Dauphine had looked to Erec as a father figure in their lonely upbringing.

Erec realized now, from her stare, and from the way she was ignoring Alistair, that after all these years she had not changed one bit.

"My brother," Dauphine said, stepping forward, embracing him, hugging him tight, refusing to let go.

Erec held her and felt her tears run down her face and onto his neck. Erec realized he'd missed his family dearly, despite all their quirks, and it was overwhelming to see them all back here in one place. In some ways, it felt as if he'd never left. It was an eerie feeling.

"My sister," he said. "I've missed you dearly."

She pulled back and looked at him.

"Not as much as I've missed you. Did you receive all my letters?"

"Every one," Erec said.

Dauphine had written to him constantly throughout the years, falcon after falcon delivering him her scrolls. Erec had replied when he could, but he was not able to write as often or as much as she. Clearly he had never been far from her thoughts, and a part of him had always felt guilty at being so far away from her, almost as if he were abandoning a daughter.

"These islands have not been the same without you," she said. "I'm sad that it took our father's impending death to bring you back. Was not I being here enough?"

Erec felt a twinge of guilt at her words, and did not know how to reply.

"I'm sorry," he finally said. "My duties compelled me elsewhere."

Erec turned to Alistair, not wanting her to feel left out, hoping that Dauphine would be gracious to her, but fearing otherwise. His stomach clenched as he introduced them.

"Dauphine, may I introduce you to my bride-to-be, Alistair."

Alistair smiled graciously, not territorial in the least, and held out a hand.

Dauphine looked at it as if a snake were being handed to her. She grimaced and turned to Erec, ignoring Alistair.

"And why do you not choose a bride from your amongst own people?" Dauphine asked. "Do you mean to have a stranger rule over us?"

Erec's face darkened, and he felt mortified with embarrassment for Alistair.

"Dauphine," he said firmly, "Alistair is my bride. I love her with all my heart. Please show her the respect that she is due. If you love me, you will love her."

Dauphine turned and stared at Alistair coldly, as if looking at an awful creature that washed up on shore. Then she suddenly turned her back and walked away, strutting off into the cheering crowd.

Erec reddened, embarrassed. That was his sister, always caught up in a storm of emotion, mostly of her own making, and always unpredictable. It was amazing; despite all the years that had passed, nothing had changed.

Erec turned to Alistair, who seemed crestfallen.

"I'm so sorry," he said. "Please forgive her. She knows not what she does. It is not personal to you."

Alistair nodded, lowering her eyes, but Erec could see that she was shaken by the reception. He felt terrible.

As he was about to console her further, the crowd parted and up stepped Erec's mother. Erec was overcome to see her. It was like having a part of himself returned.

His mother held out both hands as she stepped forward, not going to embrace Erec first, but rather Alistair. That was his mother—always unpredictable, and always having impeccable timing. She always knew exactly what to do, and when. Erec was so relieved to see her, and delighted that she had given Alistair the honor of greeting her first.

"My daughter to be," she said, holding out both hands and clasping Alistair's warmly.

Alistair looked up at her with a surprised smile, as Erec's mother hugged her, holding her tight, like a long-lost daughter. She pulled back and looked her up and down.

"Your beauty has been sung of, yet it does you no justice. For it is the most glorious thing I have ever seen. I am thrilled and delighted that Erec has chosen you for a wife. He has made many good choices in his life, but none better than this."

Alistair beamed, her eyes glistening, and Erec could see how overwhelmed she was. His heart softened. His mother had managed, once again, to undo the perpetual damage that Dauphine had done.

"Thank you, my Queen," Alistair said. "It is an honor to meet you. Any mother to Erec I shall love with all my heart."

His mother smiled back.

"Soon, you shall be his wife, and you shall be Queen. You shall hold my title. And nothing shall make me happier."

Erec's mother turned to him, and she embraced him, hugging him tight.

"Mother," he said, as she pulled back and wiped a tear from her eye. She looked so much older than when he'd left, the sight saddened him. He had been away so long, had missed so many great years of her life, and seeing her brought it all home. He saw all the new lines in her face, and he thought of his father.

"Your father awaits you," she said, as if reading his mind. "He still lives. Yet not for much longer. He does not have much time. Come now."

She took his hand, and she also took Alistair's, and together, they walked through the cheering crowd, hurrying their way, as Erec braced himself, anxious to see his father in his dying moments. No matter what happened, he was home.

He was *home*.

# CHAPTER SIXTEEN

Gwendolyn rode in the wagon at the rear of her people, trekking west and south alongside the Canyon, as they had been all day, heading for the crossing. Gwen took comfort in knowing that, despite her people's protest, soon they would be across the Canyon and that much closer to boarding the fleet of ships waiting to take them to the Upper Isles. Her heart tugged with a combination of remorse and urgency, knowing it was the right thing to do, yet still hating to do it.

Most of all, though, Gwen stirred with uneasiness as she looked out at her people, the thousands and thousands who had marched from King's Court reluctantly, resentfully, all under the eyes of her watchful soldiers who bordered the people on every side and kept them marching along. It was like a controlled riot. Her people clearly did not want to go, and Gwen heard them grumbling louder at every turn. She didn't know how much longer she could control them; it was like a storm waiting to break.

"Ruling is not always painless," said a voice beside her.

Gwen looked over to see Kendrick riding up alongside her on his horse, proudly, nobly, Sandara, his new love, mounted on his horse behind him.

Gwen took comfort at seeing him. She smiled, tense.

"Father would always say that," Gwen replied.

Kendrick smiled back.

"You are doing what you think is best for your people."

"But you don't agree," Gwen said.

Kendrick shrugged.

"That is not important. I admire that you are doing it."

"But still you don't agree with my actions," she pressed.

Kendrick sighed.

"Sometimes you and Argon see things that I don't. It is not something I understand well. I never have. I am a knight; I aspire for

103

little else. I do not have your skill or talent for seeing into things; I am not comfortable with other realms. But I trust you. I always have. Father trusted you, too, and that is enough for me. In fact, our beloved father chose you for precisely times like this."

Gwendolyn looked at him, touched.

"You're the greatest brother I could want," she said. "You have always been there for me. Even when you don't agree."

Kendrick smiled back at her.

"You're my sister. And my Queen. I would go to the ends of the earth for you—whether I agree with you or not."

There came a shout, and Gwendolyn turned to see a group of people angrily shoving the soldiers who were keeping them moving along the evacuation route. She sensed what little order they had was starting to break down, and she was starting to wonder how she would ever get her people across the Canyon. Indeed, as their shouting escalated, she wondered if there might even be an outright rebellion against her.

They rounded a bend, and Gwendolyn's breath stopped as she looked out and saw the vastness of the Canyon spread out before her. She saw all the layers of mist, all different colors, lingering in the air, saw the endless expanse, which seemed to reach into the very heavens themselves. And she saw the magnificent bridge spanning it, waiting for them.

As her people reached the base of the crossing, suddenly, they came to a stop. The shouting escalated, and she could see that her men were no longer able to control the masses, who swayed about, to and fro, like caged animals. The people absolutely refused to take one more step forward, onto the bridge. She could see that they were afraid to cross it.

"We will not leave the Ring!" a man shouted.

The crowd cheered.

"Our home is here! If there is to be danger here, then we will die here," another shouted.

Another cheer.

"You cannot make us go!" another shouted.

There arose a chorus of cheers, as her people became increasingly emboldened.

Gwendolyn knew she had to do something. She stood on her cart, high above the masses, and held out her hands for silence.

Slowly, her people quieted, as all eyes turned to her.

"No," she boomed out, "I cannot make you go. You are right. But I am your Queen, and I ask this of you. I promise you, there is good cause. And I promise you, that if you stay here, you will die."

The crowd jeered, heckling her, and Gwendolyn's cheeks flushed, as she felt what it was like to be hated as a ruler. For the first time, she wished she was not Queen.

"To King's Court!" a man screamed.

The people turned and began to head back in her direction, away from the bridge. She saw her men losing control, saw that they could not stop them.

As Gwen stood there, heart pounding in her chest, clutching Guwayne, wondering what to do next, there came a sudden horrific shriek in the sky, one loud enough to make the hairs stand up on the back of Gwen's neck.

Her people stopped shouting and instead stood there, looking up to the skies. Gwen turned and looked east, toward the horizon, already having a sinking feeling of what it could be.

*No, Gwen thought. Not now. Not when we're so close to leaving.*

There was another screech, then another, and then another. She knew this screech anywhere. It was a primordial cry, the most powerful cry in the world.

It was the cry of a dragon.

# CHAPTER SEVENTEEN

Reece sat in the hold of the Queen's ship, the sound of the rain slamming against the wood filling the air, his back against the wall, nursing his leg wound and happy to be alive. Beside him sat Stara, Srog, and Matus, drinking hot ale and nursing their wounds, each of them tended by one of the Queen's healers. Reece grimaced as a healer sewed up the gash on his thigh left after she'd pulled out the arrow. It stung, but he was relieved the arrow was out, and relieved that he had taken it while protecting Stara.

Beside him Stara was taking her stitches bravely, barely even wincing, her healer finishing up with the last stitch, then applying various salves. Reece felt a cold sting as his healer draped a cold cloth on his leg filled with ointments; he felt the cool gels slowly infiltrate his wound. After a few seconds, it brought relief, and he relaxed and began to feel better.

Reece took another long drink from his ale, the hot liquid feeling good on this cold and rainy night, and going right to his head. He could not remember he had last eaten. As he sat there, Reece felt incredibly relaxed after the harrowing events of the night, and grateful that they had reached the ship against all odds. Reece realized how lucky they were to have escaped with relatively minor wounds. Even Srog, the most wounded, was now receiving the healing he needed, and for the first time, Reece saw the color returning to his cheeks, as several healers worked on his injuries and assured him he would be okay.

Sitting opposite them all was Wolfson, Commander of the Queen's fleet, a grizzled warrior with a beard streaked with gray, a lazy eye, and the broad and hardened face of a warrior. He wore the uniform of a Queen's sailor, adorned with all the medals and honors befitting his rank. He was a fine commander, Reece knew, one who had served his father through many wars at sea. Reece was relieved that they had reached his ship.

As soon as they had all boarded, Reece had warned Wolfson immediately of the fiery arrows being prepared that would set his fleet aflame as soon as the rain stopped. Wolfson had jumped into action, raising the anchors for his entire fleet and sailing them further out to sea, out of range of any arrows from shore.

Now here they all sat, anchored nearly a mile offshore, in rougher ocean waters, getting slammed by the rain, the ship rocking in the waves. Again and again, they had gone over the details of what had happened, and what next steps they must take.

"You saved us all this night," Wolfson said. "If it were not for you all, we would have been caught by surprise, and our ships would all be aflame as soon as the rain stopped."

"And yet we are still not safe here," Matus said. "We are safe from arrows, yes, but do not think the Upper Islanders will rest on their heels. At first light, my brother Karus will summon his fleet from the far side of the island, and he will attack what remains of your fleet at open sea. They have dozens more ships than you, and you'll be exposed here in the open water."

"Nor can you set foot on shore, with the army waiting for you," Srog added.

Wolfson nodded, as if he had already thought it through.

"Then we shall go down fighting," he replied.

"Why wait for morning?" Stara asked. "Why wait for them to ambush us and attack us in the open sea? Why not set sail right now for the Ring?"

Wolfson shook his head.

"The last order Queen MacGil gave me was to keep our fleet here in this bay, and to hold our positions. I have no order otherwise. I will not abandon our post. Not unless the Queen orders me to retreat."

"That's craziness," Stara said.

Srog sighed.

"We are soldiers," he said. "Queen MacGil ordered us to hold his island. We do not defy the chain of command."

"And yet she does not know the circumstances that have occurred here," Stara pointed out. "After all, she did not expect her brother to kill King Tirus and spark a revolution."

Reece saw everyone look at him, and he reddened. He wondered if Stara was deliberately taking a dig at him, and if she hated him for killing her father.

"He was a traitor," Reece said, "he deserved death."

"Even so, your actions sparked a war," she countered. "I think your Queen would understand our retreat."

Wolfson shook his head.

"Without a direct order, we do not retreat."

All eyes turned to Srog, the Queen's official voice on the island. After a long while he sighed, resigned. He shook his head.

"I have no orders otherwise," he said. "We cannot abandon our posts. We stay put and fight."

The men all nodded and grunted in satisfaction, all in agreement. They dug in, surveying their weapons, preparing mentally for the inevitable fight that would come in the morning.

Srog and Matus joined Wolfson as he crossed the room, on a mission for more ale, each of them limping but gaining their feet, and Reece found himself alone with Stara, sitting side by side, nursing a hot cup of ale. Reece set down his mug and removed a stone from his belt and began sharpening his sword. He did not know what to say to Stara, or whether she even wanted to talk to him, so they sat there in the silence, the sound of the sword sharpening cutting gently through the room.

Reece assumed that Stara was mad at him, probably over Selese, or probably over his killing her father, and he expected her to get up and cross the room with the others; he was surprised that she continued to sit there, a few feet away. Reece did not know what to feel around her; a part of him felt shame when he looked at her, thinking of Selese, and also of how he had broken his vow to return for her. He felt guilty even looking at her, given his incredible love and grief for Selese, which hung over him like a blanket. He felt a storm of emotions, and he did not know what to think. A part of him did not want to see her, given what had happened with Selese.

Yet another part of him, he had to admit, wanted her to stay close. A part of him wanted her to talk to him, wanted things to go back to the way they used to be. But he felt guilty even thinking that.

Clearly, Reece had messed everything up, in every direction. Stara probably hated him, and he could not blame her.

"Thank you for saving me back there," Stara finally spoke up, her voice so soft Reece was unsure he'd even heard it.

Reece turned and looked at her, shocked, wondering if she had really spoken the words, or if he had just imagined them. Stara was looking down to the floor, not at him, her knees bent up to her chest, looking forlorn.

"I didn't save you," he said.

She turned and looked at him, her eyes aglow, filled with intensity; he was struck, as always, by how hypnotizing they were.

"You did," she said. "You took the arrows for me."

Reece shrugged.

"I owe you as much as you do me," he replied. "If not more. You've saved me several times now."

Reece went back to sharpening his sword, and she looked back at the floor, and they fell back into a silence, albeit this time a more comfortable one. Reece was surprised that she had spoken to him, and that she did not seem to harbor any ill feelings for him.

"I thought you hated me," Reece said, after a while.

She turned and looked at him.

"Hated you?" she asked, her voice rising in surprise.

Reece turned to look at her.

"After all, I killed your father."

Stara scoffed.

"That is all the more reason to like you," she said. "It was long overdue. I'm surprised I did not kill him myself."

Reece looked at her, shocked. It was not the answer he had been expecting.

"Then you must…hate me for other reasons," Reece said.

Stara gazed at him, puzzled.

"And what might those reasons be?"

Reece sighed.

"I vowed to come back to you," he said, getting it off his chest. "I vowed to call off my wedding to Selese. And I broke my vow. I let you down. And for that, I am ashamed."

Stara sighed.

"I was disappointed, of course. I thought our love was true. I was disappointed to find out that it was not. That your words were empty."

"But my words were *not* empty," Reece insisted.

She looked at him, baffled.

"Then why did you change your mind and decide to marry Selese after all?"

Reece sighed, confused, not knowing what to say. His mind raced with conflicting emotions.

"It's not that I did not love you," he said. "It's that I realized that I also loved Selese. Perhaps in a different way. Perhaps even not as strongly as I loved you. But I loved her all the same. And I had given her my word. And as I sailed back, as distance came between us, I realized it was a word I had to keep."

She frowned.

"And what of your word to me?" she asked. "And what of your love for me? Did that mean nothing, then?"

Reece shook his head, not knowing what to say.

"It meant a great deal," he finally said. "And I know I broke your heart. I'm sorry."

Stara shrugged.

"I guess it's all too late for that now," she said. "You made your choice. Your wife-to-be, the one you had decided to dedicate the rest of your life to, is dead. And I'm sure you blame me for it."

Reece considered her words, wondering if they were true. Did he really blame her? A part of him did. But a deeper part of him knew that he himself was the only one to blame.

"I blame myself more than you," he replied, "much more. It was my choice. Not yours."

Reece sighed.

"And as you said, none of that matters now," he added. "When Selese died, a part of me died with her. I vowed to never love again. And it is a vow that, this time, I intend to keep."

Stara looked at him, and he watched her face transform, watched her become crushed, once again. He could see something gloss over her eyes, like a severe disappointment. A resignation. He realized in that moment that she still loved him, was still hoping for them to be together. And he had, unwittingly, hurt her once again.

Stara suddenly nodded, then got up wordlessly and walked away.

Reece looked down, sharpening his sword, hating himself even more and trying to push it all out of his mind; but Stara's footsteps, crossing the deck, echoed in his skull as she went farther and farther away, each step like a nail in the coffin of his heart.

# CHAPTER EIGHTEEN

Gwen stood at the base of the Canyon and watched the horizon, frozen in terror, as slowly, out of the clouds, there emerged a host of dragons, huge, ancient, all breathing fire as they closed in on them. The screeches cut through the air again and again, shaking the ground, so intense that Gwen had to raise her hands to her ears. Watching them approach was like watching a nightmare come to life, and Gwen had the surreal experience of seeing the actual doom arrive that she had foreseen for so many moons.

All around her, all of her people, so reluctant to cross the Canyon just moments before, suddenly burst into screams, turned, and ran for their lives, sprinting across the very bridge they had protested against. They ran for the lives to get as far away from the Ring as possible, taking, ironically, the same route that Gwen had wanted them to take all along.

But now, it was too late. Gwen had been proven right. She had been right all along. But she felt little satisfaction.

The dragons dove down, closer and closer, breathing fire. As a wall of flame approached, Gwen, already feeling the heat, knew that in just moments, she, and everyone she knew and loved, would be dead.

Beside her stood all of her councilors, and behind her stood all of her knights, the faithful Silver, to their credit, none of them running, all standing beside her, holding up the rear to protect their people. Behind her, in the distance, she could hear the shouts of thousands of her people, running for their lives. If only they had listened to her earlier, Gwen thought. They would all be on ships by now, out to sea, on their way to safety.

The dragons dove down in a fury, and Gwen knew that despite her people's best efforts, soon they would all be dead—not just her, but everyone who tried to flee across the bridge. Dragons were too quick, too strong, too powerful. Nothing in the world could stop them.

Gwen looked up and watched them get near, monstrous, beautiful creatures, their wings flapping, their immense teeth showing, and she knew that she was staring death in the face. She had only one regret before she died—that her love, Thorgrin, was not here, by her side. She wished to see him one more time.

Gwendolyn clutched Guwayne tightly, holding his face to her chest, not wanting him to see this. She wished, too, that Guwayne could be far from here, anywhere but here, safe in another world. His life was too short, and too precious, to end this way.

The dragons approached, their shrieks deafening, now so close that Gwendolyn could feel the hair on her skin bristling from the heat. Her men stood bravely beside her, but Gwen knew it was a futile effort. The wall of flame would melt their swords before they even had a chance to raise them.

Gwendolyn closed her eyes and prepared to meet her fate.

*Please, God. You can take me. Just allow my people to safety. And my baby. Please. I offer myself up. Just save them.*

When Gwen opened her eyes she was surprised to hear a roar. It was a distinct roar, one different from the other dragons, one she knew well. It was a roar she'd become accustomed to hearing every day, and a roar she had not heard since the day that Mycoples had left.

Ralibar.

Gwendolyn looked up to see her old friend Ralibar fast approaching, flying over the Canyon from the west, racing to confront the oncoming dragons, a fury in his face unlike any she had ever seen. Ralibar, larger than them all, a loner, was a fearsome dragon to behold, even more fearsome than those approaching, and he was fearless as he faced an army by himself.

All the dragons suddenly stopped breathing fire, stopped looking down at Gwen and the others, and instead they changed their focus, looking up to Ralibar. They flew faster and prepared to vanquish him.

There came a tremendous crashing noise overhead, as Ralibar smashed into the lead dragon, his talons out; Ralibar leaned back and wrapped his talons around the dragon's throat, and then continued flying, driving the dragon back, farther and farther, like a cannonball through the air. Then Ralibar dove down, before the other dragons could reach him, and smashed the dragon down to the ground, the entire earth shaking as they tumbled.

The other dragons turned around to aid their friend.

"We must go!" Kendrick yelled out beside her, tugging on her sleeve. "Now, my Queen!"

Gwendolyn knew he was right; this was their chance to flee. And yet she hated to leave Ralibar all alone like that—especially as all the other dragons turned and dove down to attack him.

Yet still, Gwen knew she had no choice; there was nothing she could do to help defend Ralibar. Even if she tried to help him, it would be futile. And this was her only chance to escape, while the dragons were distracted.

"Now, my Queen!" Kendrick implored, yanking her arm.

Gwen finally turned and joined her men, all of them mounting their horses and carriages and charging across the bridge.

They soon joined their people, thousands of them continuing their mass exodus across the bridge, and finally onto the other side of the Ring. They reached the Wilds, and Gwen thought of the road ahead, and thanked God she had the fleet awaiting them at the shores for the evacuation.

Her people fled in a mass panic, and none of them stopped to look back. None, that is, except for Gwendolyn. As she reached the far side of the crossing, Gwen turned to take one last look, and her heart sank to see Ralibar being attacked from all sides. Ralibar fought brilliantly, pinning down one dragon after the next, using his talons, slashing, wrestling, using his great teeth, locking onto their throats. He fought viciously, taking down one dragon after the next.

But there were just too many of them, and they attacked him from all sides. One after the other, they dove down at him, like angry birds, grabbing him, throwing him, clawing and biting, smashing him into boulders. Ralibar fought valiantly, but soon he was being pounded into the ground by one dragon after the next.

"Gwendolyn, GO!" suddenly commanded a firm voice that she recognized.

Gwendolyn looked over in shock to see Argon, and she wondered how he got there.

Argon walked alone, fearlessly, out onto the bridge by himself. He wore an intense expression, focused on Ralibar, and Gwen watched, transfixed, as Argon marched out to the center of the bridge, using his staff. He finally stopped, held out a single palm, and aimed east, toward Ralibar and the others.

"Ralibar, I summon you," Argon boomed, his voice ancient, commanding. "Return to me!"

Ralibar, on the ground, tumbling, getting pinned down again and again, turned his head and looked toward the sound of Argon's voice.

Suddenly, from Argon's raised palm there emerged a brilliant white light, shooting across the bridge to the edge of the Canyon. As it did, it morphed into a huge wall of white light, rising from the ground to the heavens, clinging to the side of the Canyon. It looked as if Argon were single-handedly creating a new energy shield.

Ralibar suddenly rolled out from under the other dragons, got to his feet, and flapped his great wings. He lifted into the sky, the other dragons on his tail, and headed toward Argon. He was wounded, not flying as fast as he usually did, and a dragon managed to catch him, biting his tail. Gwen held her breath as she feared Ralibar might not make it.

But Ralibar broke free, flapping harder and harder, and he broke away just long enough to fly through Argon's wall of light, back into the air across the Canyon.

The other dragons followed right behind him, but as soon as they hit the light wall, they smashed headfirst into it. They screamed in fury, smashing into it again and again, but they were unable to penetrate it.

Argon stood, both palms raised now, creating and maintaining the energy shield, and his arms trembled. Gwen had never seen him under so much strain; he seemed to feel pain every time the dragons hit the shield. Soon, Argon collapsed from the effort, and Gwen cried out as she watched him hit the ground. Argon lay there, helpless, curled up in a ball, at the center of the bridge.

"Ralibar!" Gwen shouted, pointing.

Ralibar turned at the sound of her voice, and he looked down and saw Argon's body; Ralibar let out a cry and he dove down, his talons extended, aiming right for Argon. He swooped him up, clutching him tight, and flew with him, carrying him higher and higher up in the air.

He followed Gwendolyn as she turned, leading him and all of her people on the road before them, through the Wilds, for her ships, and for a place anywhere in the world that was not the Ring.

# CHAPTER NINETEEN

Thorgrin trekked through the endless fields of mud in the Land of the Druids, looking out at the horizon and hoping to see something, anything; instead, there was nothing but desolation, nothing to break up the monotony of the landscape, which seemed to stretch forever. Dark clouds glowered, hung low in the air, low enough to nearly touch, completing the picture of gloom.

It was the exact picture of the Underworld that Thor remembered, when he had been marching through the wasteland of the Empire. Yet Thor forced himself to remember, to know that he was not in the Empire. He was in the Land of the Druids, he told himself. All that he saw before him was a creation of his mind. He was not walking through a landscape, he knew, but walking through the contours of his own mind.

Consciously, Thor knew it to be true, and he wanted to stop it, to change the picture before him, to think happy thoughts; but oddly, he found himself unable to change it. He did not, he realized, have the power to do so yet. As much as he tried to will a different landscape, a different world, he found himself trekking through this one, his feet sticking to the mud with each step he took, each step labored, his breathing hard. And he felt a deeper sense of foreboding the farther he went, as if he could be attacked at any moment. By what, he did not know.

Thor reached for his weapons, but looked down to find his belt empty; in fact, he was no longer wearing armor. He was dressed in rags again, in the simple frock of a shepherd's boy that he used to wear. What had happened? How was he dressed like this again? Where had his weapons gone? As Thor felt around his waistband, all he found was a simple sling, the one from his childhood, well worn from years of use.

117

Thor marched and marched, on guard, and felt that this was a training ground, that his subconscious was taking him through stages of his life. As he squinted into the horizon, he began to see something come into view. It appeared to be a forest of some sort, and as he approached, he saw that it was a new landscape, filled with dead trees as far as the eye could see, their branches black, twisted. It was a massive orchard of death.

Thor walked down a narrow path leading him into this forest, beneath the gnarled branches of all the trees, the skies filled with the sounds of crows, and as he went, he spotted something that put a pit in his stomach: from a nearby tree, he saw a figure hanging, dressed in armor, swaying even though there was no wind. His rusted armor creaked as he swayed, and as the faceplate fell, Thor recognized him: it was Kolk, his former commander of the Legion, a noose about his neck.

Thor wanted to bring him down, to help him, but as he neared, he saw his eyes wide open, saw that he was long dead. Puzzled, Thor continued to walk, wondering. At the next tree, he spotted another hanging body, swaying, eyes wide open. It was Conven, his former Legion brother.

As Thor continued on, he saw thousands of knights in rusted armor, hanging from the trees; as he passed, he saw that each tree held a different body, all of them people he once knew, people he once fought with. There were people he knew to be dead; then, Thor was shocked to see, there were people he knew to still be alive: Reece, Elden, O'Connor. All of his Legion brothers. Then came members of the Silver. All of them dead.

"You are the last one left."

Thor turned and looked all around for the source of the voice, but he could not find it.

"A warrior learns to fight alone. His men are all around him. But his battlefield is himself."

Thor turned again and again, but still he could not find the voice. It was Argon's voice, he knew; yet he was nowhere in sight.

Thor hurried down the trail, past the thousands of swinging bodies, feeling as if the entire world were dead, and wondering if this would ever end. As he thought it, suddenly the forest disappeared, and he was back in the desolate landscape of mud.

Thor heard a whooshing noise, and he looked down to see something slithering beneath the surface of the mud, which became translucent. He looked closely and saw a gigantic snake, just beneath the surface, rushing past. As he studied the ground, he suddenly saw thousands of exotic creatures, all slithering a few inches beneath the surface of the mud. Somehow, they were not able to puncture the surface of the mud, yet Thor felt as if it any moment, he might fall through and be immersed into a pit of death.

Thor closed his eyes as he walked.

*These creatures are not real,* he told himself. *They are creatures that slither beneath the surface of my consciousness. I created them. I can suppress them. Use your mind, Thorgrin. Use your mind.*

Thor felt a tremendous heat rise between his eyes, in the center of his forehead, and he felt himself getting stronger and stronger. He felt himself controlling the fabric of the universe around him.

Thor opened his eyes and looked down, and he blinked in surprise to see the creatures were gone. He was now walking on nothing but mud.

Thorgrin felt empowered, beginning to realize he had the ability, after all, to summon his powers, to control his environment. He was beginning to understand how to harness it, how to reach into the deeper levels of himself; he was beginning to understand that there was no distinction between the world inside his mind and the world outside.

He was also starting to realize that this entire land was a training ground. He realized he had to reach a certain level before he could face his mother. Before he was worthy.

A thick fog rolled through as Thor walked, momentarily blinding him. As it finally lifted, he peered through and in the distance, he saw a single object rising out of the mud. The fog rolled in again, and he

119

wasn't certain if he saw it, and he increased his pace, eager to see what it was.

Thor got closer, and as he did, the fog lifted again and he saw it again. He stopped before it, scrutinizing it, wondering. At first, it appeared to be a giant cross; but as he reached out to touch it, he realized it was something else. It was caked in mud, layers of mud, and as he reached out, he wiped it off, bit by bit. Slowly, a piece of the object came into view: it was a glistening hilt, studded with jewels.

Thor stood there, frozen, his breath catching in his throat. He could not believe it. Standing before him, its blade lodged into the earth, caked in layers of mud, waiting for him to grab it, was the Destiny Sword.

Thor blinked several times, wondering. It felt so real. He knew it was real. And yet, at the same time, Thor knew that he had created this, along with everything else in this land. It felt so good to see this weapon again, to have his old friend back again, a weapon that he had crossed half the world for, had lost a dear friend for, that had dictated so much of his journey in life. Wielding the Destiny Sword had meant more to Thor than he could say. He nearly cried at the sight of it; he realized how much he had missed it. Indeed, he had been haunted by dreams of its being just out of his reach ever since the day he had lost it.

And now as he saw it here, he realized it was his dreams that were creating this. The deepest levels of his subconscious.

Thor reached out, grabbed the hilt of sword, and pulled, expecting to easily extract it from the mud.

Yet Thor was shocked when it did not budge.

Thor pulled harder, then grasped it with both hands. The sword rocked back and forth, but no matter how hard he tried, he was unable to extract it.

Thorgrin finally shouted out with effort, then collapsed, dropping to his knees, breathing hard, crushed.

How could it be? How could it be possible that he was no longer worthy of wielding this sword?

"You were never as strong as you thought, Thornicus," came a dark voice.

The hairs rose on the back of Thor's neck as he instantly realized whose voice it was.

He turned slowly and saw the man he hated most in the world standing there, facing him, an evil smile across his face:

Andronicus.

Andronicus grinned down at him, holding a huge battle-ax in one hand and a sword in the other. His muscles were bulging, his armor barely able to contain them, as he loomed over Thor.

"What are you doing here?" Thor asked. "How did you get here?"

Andronicus laughed, an awful, grating sound.

"I came to this land just like you," he replied. "Searching. I was searching for greater power, for my innermost power. I was a young warrior. And that was when I met your mother."

Thor stared back, shocked.

"I told you I would come back to you in your dreams," Andronicus said. "And here, in this land, dreams are real enough to kill you."

Andronicus lunged forward with his ax and Thor dodged at the last moment as the ax brushed by, just missing him.

"You are not real!" Thor yelled out, aiming a palm at his father, trying to summon his power to make him go away.

Andronicus swung his sword and sliced Thor's arm.

Thor cried out in horrific pain, blood gushing from the wound.

Andronicus looked back, laughing.

"Is that not real? When I stab you through the heart, you'll be dead, for all time. Just like me. You may have created me. But now I am here, and I am real enough to kill you—and I will."

Andronicus swung again and again, and Thor dodged each time, the sword just missing, but each time getting closer. Thor looked over at the Destiny Sword and wished more than anything that he could wield it.

121

As Andronicus bore down on him, Thor remembered his sling: he reached down, grabbed it, and hurled a stone.

The stone went sailing for Andronicus head, but Andronicus swung his sword and swatted the stone out of the air.

"Your boyhood weapons will do you no good here, boy," his father said.

Thor desperately searched for a weapon anywhere, but he could find none. He was defenseless against this monster, and Andronicus was determined to kill him.

"You still resist me," Andronicus said. "But I am a part of you. Accept me. Accept me, and I will disappear."

"Never!" Thor exclaimed.

Andronicus raised his ax and threw it at Thor. Thor had not expected it, and he barely had time to dodge as it flew end over end, and sliced his shoulder. Thor yelled out in pain, as blood squirted from his other arm.

Before he could react, Andronicus kicked him with both feet in the chest, knocking Thor down on his back.

Thor slid dozens of feet on the mud, until he finally came to a stop. He looked up, but Andronicus already stood over him, and raised his battle-ax high.

"I love you, Thornicus. And that is why I must kill you."

As Andronicus raised his ax high, Thor, defenseless, raised his hands and shouted out, knowing this would be an awful way to die.

## CHAPTER TWENTY

Erec quickly climbed the endless stairs leading to the top of the highest peak of the Southern Isles, looking up as he went, his heart warmed at the sight of his father's fort. There it sat, on the highest point of the island, just as he'd remembered as a child. It was a beautiful structure, like a small castle, yet square and low to the ground, adorned with turrets and parapets. It was built of ancient stones quarried centuries ago from these cliffs, and its presence was imposing. For Erec, it was home; yet it also embodied a special place in his dreams, an almost magical place.

Erec approached its massive copper doors, tall and rectangular, shining so brightly in the sun he had to squint, with their huge carved handles that brought back memories. Erec had forgotten that the Southern Isles were a land of copper, its bountiful copper mines yielding an endless amount of material, so much so that nearly every structure in the Southern Isles, even the poorest house, had some element of copper in it. His father's fort, the most beautiful and elaborate structure here, had so much copper on it, shined so brightly, that it was visible from nearly any point on the islands. It was designed to leave people in awe—whether friends or enemies.

Erec was breathing hard, his legs burning, as he finally reached the plateau and approached the place—he had forgotten how steep the Upper Isles were, how the entire island was basically one huge mountain range, a series of elevations, rising and falling, people constantly having to climb endless steps carved into the stone to reach anything. His father's fort, most of all. Erec realized that, whatever shape he was in, it was still not the shape of the Southern Islanders, where all the men—and women—had legs of tree trunks, accustomed their entire lives to climbing and descending.

As Erec approached the doors, Alistair at his side, half a dozen soldiers, dressed in the uniform of the Southern Isles, head to toe in copper armor, weapons, shields, shining like the fort, immediately stepped aside and pulled open the doors for him. They bowed their heads low, offering him a reception fit for a king. It gave Erec a strange sensation; it brought home the fact that soon, his father would be dead—and he would be King.

Erec had never been treated like a king before, and he realized he did not like the feeling. He was a humble man at heart, his entire life devoted to being a loyal soldier, a warrior, a knight—not to politics or pomp. His life was devoted to serving others, to serving the Ring, to be the best warrior he could be. He cared for little else.

Seeing all these people in the Southern Isles treat him with such a reception made him realize that his life was about to change. He would soon be spending less time with his weaponry, less time in the field, and more time being a ruler, in halls of politics. He was not sure if he liked the feeling. Was that the natural evolution of a warrior? he wondered. To rise up from the field of battle, a place of honor, and to enter into the murky field of politics? Erec felt that there more honor in battle, and that the deeper one waded into the politics and power, the more one risked one's honor. Was evolving from warrior to ruler the natural evolution of responsibility? Or was it a de-evolution, a tarnishing of one's honors and virtues?

Erec did not know the answer, and a part of him did not want to find out. He wanted a simple life as a warrior, defending his kingdom, living amongst his people. He did not want to rule them. And yet he was his father's firstborn, and everyone on the Isles, including his father, would expect nothing less of him.

If there was any saving grace to being King on these isles, it was that Kings here were different from Kings anywhere else in the world; to be King here meant that one not only had to picked by lineage—one also had to earn it. To earn the Kingship, Erec would have to be tested on the field of battle, by his own people. A contest would be called, and any commoner would have the right to challenge him. If any one of them defeated him, then the Kingship would pass to them. At least Erec, assuming he won, would be King through merit—and not through lineage alone.

Erec marched down the corridors holding Alistair's hand, their footsteps echoing off the copper floors, attendants and soldiers lined up, bowing their heads as they passed. More attendants opened another set of doors for them, and they turned down another corridor, and another, and finally, before them were the doors to his father's chamber. One last soldier opened the door, and Erec braced himself, nervous, anticipating what state his father might be in.

Alistair stopped with him before the door, tugging his hand.

"My lord, shall I enter with you?" Alistair asked, hesitant.

Erec nodded.

"You shall be my wife. It is fitting that you meet my father before he dies."

"Yet you have not seen him since your youth. Perhaps you want some time alone with him."

Erec clutched her hand. "Where I go, you go."

The two entered the room and the door closed behind them, leaving just the two of them in this room with the King, along with the attendants lined up solemnly along the walls.

For the first time since he was a boy, Erec laid eyes on his father, and his heart sank. His father lay in bed, head propped up on silk pillows, silk covers up to his chest despite the warm summer day. He looked so much older, frailer, smaller than Erec remembered. The sight pained him to no end.

In Erec's memory, his father was as a tall, broad-chested great warrior, a fierce and tough man, wise and calculating, respected by all who looked at him. He was a man who had managed to grasp the throne in his youth, to out-fight others who had royal lineage by sheer strength, determination, and fighting skill.

As he was a warrior and not a ruler, a man who did not hail from royal blood, all the islanders had been certain that he would not be able to hang onto the throne, and would not be a great ruler. But his father surprised them all. He turned out to be not only the best warrior in the Isles, but also a great and cunning ruler. He managed to hold onto the throne—and strengthen it—his entire life, and in the process, made the Southern Isles a much stronger place. He was the one who had discovered the copper mines, who had brought them all wealth, who had helped build most of the copper structures on the island today; he was the one who had extended the fishing fleet, had reinforced the cliffs, had made the islands prosperous and bountiful—and who had fended off all attacks on his islands. He had succeeded all these years, despite the predictions, and he had, unpredictably, become the greatest King the Southern Isles had ever known.

And now he lay dying, this mountain of a man, and Erec knew there would be huge shoes to fill. He did not know if he, or anyone, was capable of filling them.

"Father," Erec said, his heart breaking as he stepped forward and stopped by his father's bedside.

The King opened his eyes slightly, then at the sight of Erec, opened them more widely. He leaned his head forward, just a little, looked at Erec, and reached out a frail hand.

Erec clasped it and kissed his father's hand. It was wrinkly and old and cold to the touch. It felt like death.

"My son," he said, longing in his voice.

Erec admired his father as a king and as a soldier; but he had mixed feelings about him as a father. After all, his father had shipped him off at a very young age, had sent him away from everything he knew and loved. He knew his father did it for his benefit, but nonetheless, a part of Erec felt as if his father did not want him here. Or was more interested in being a king than a father.

A part of Erec, he couldn't deny, would have liked to stay here, to be close, to spend his life with his father and his family; a part of Erec, he had to admit, resented his father for this forced exile, for choosing his life for him.

"You have reached me before my death," his father said.

Erec nodded, his eyes glistening at the sound of his father's weak voice. It did not seem fitting that such a great warrior should be reduced to this.

"Perhaps you shall not die, Father," he said.

His father shook his head.

"Every healer here has seen me twice. I was supposed to die months ago. I have hung on," he said, breaking into a fit of coughing, "to see you."

Erec could see his father's eyes glistening, and he could see that his father did indeed care about him. It struck his heart deeply. Despite himself, Erec felt a tear form. He quickly wiped it away.

"You probably believe I did not care about you, having sent you away all these years. But it is because I *did* care about you. I knew that a life with the MacGils would gain you fame and reputation and rank beyond what you could ever have achieved here, on our small islands. As a boy, you were the finest warrior I had ever seen. Dare I say, I saw myself in you. It is true, I did not want to deprive the MacGils of your skills; but between you and I, I will tell you, it was also that I did not want to deprive you of the power you could achieve there."

Erec nodded, touched, beginning to understand, to look at his father in a whole new light.

"I understand, Father."

His father broke into another fit of coughing, and when he stopped, he looked up and saw Alistair. He waved her over.

"Your bride," he said. "I want to see her."

Erec turned and nodded and Alistair stepped forward tentatively, then kneeled beside Erec, reached out, and kissed his father's hand.

"My liege," she said softly.

He looked her up and down, carefully, for a long time, then finally nodded with satisfaction.

"You are far more than just a beautiful woman," he said. "I can see it in your eyes. You are a warrior, too. Erec has chosen well."

Alistair nodded back, seeming to be touched.

"Treat him well," the King added. "You will be Queen here one day soon. A Queen must be more than a devoted wife. Treat my people well, too. People need a King—but they also need a Queen. Do not forget that."

Alistair nodded.

"Yes, my liege."

"I must talk to you now," he said to Erec.

Erec nodded to Alistair, and she bowed and quickly turned and left the room, closing the door behind her.

"All of you, leave us," the King called out.

127

One by one his flock of attendants hurried from the room, closing the door.

Erec and his father were left alone, and the silence felt heavier. Erec clutched his father's hand, freely allowing a tear to roll down his face.

"I do not want you to die, Father," he said, holding back tears.

"I know, my son. Yet my time has come to an end on this earth. Few things matter to me now. What matters to me now, most of all, is you."

He coughed for a long time, then leaned forward.

"Listen to me," he commanded, his voice suddenly firm, bearing the strength Erec remembered as a child. He looked up and saw a glimmer of the fierce determination in his father's face that he recalled. "There's much you must understand, and not much time to learn it. My people—our people— they are more complex than you think. Never forget our roots. Hundreds of years ago, our islands were a mere colony for prisoners, outcasts, exiles, slaves—all the people that the Ring did not want. They shipped them here to die.

"But we surprised them all, and we survived. We became a people in our own right. And over centuries, we have evolved. We have become self-sufficient, and the greatest warriors anywhere in the Empire. We have become adept sailors, fishermen, farmers, even in these rugged cliffs. Now, centuries later, we have gone from outcasts to a crown jewel, a nation of bounty and warriors.

"Our relationship with the MacGils mended over the years to the point where we sent them our warriors to apprentice and they sent us theirs. The MacGils want our warriors. There's always been an unspoken alliance between us. In times of great trouble or danger, they expect us to come to their aid. But what you must understand is that our people are divided. Some consider us indebted to them, and will remain loyal to the death. But a good deal of us are isolationists. They resent the Ring, and do not want to help."

He looked at Erec meaningfully.

"You must understand your people. If you try to rally them all to the defense of the Ring, you may have a civil war on your hands. They

128

are proud, and stubborn. Try to lead them all, and you will lead none of them. You must lead carefully. Do you understand? It is you as King who must decide."

His father broke into a prolonged fit of coughing, and Erec sat there, trying to process it all. He was beginning to realize that his people and their politics were much more complex than he'd thought.

"But Father, the MacGil family took me in as one of theirs. The Ring is my second home. I have sworn to come to their aid if ever they needed it—and I always keep my vows."

His father nodded.

"And now you will come to realize what it means to be a King. It is easy to give your word—and to keep it—as a warrior; it is much harder to keep it as a ruler. If your people will not follow you, who exactly are you ruling?"

Erec thought of his words, as his father suddenly closed his eyes. He lifted his hand and waved Erec off. Erec wanted to say goodbye to him, to hug him.

But that was not his father's way—it never was. His father was a cold and hard man when he wanted to be—even abrupt. And now Erec could see that he was through with him. Erec had served his purpose.

As Erec turned to walk out the door, his father coughing and coughing, Erec knew this was the last time he'd ever see him, and he was left wondering. His father had left him as heir to his kingdom—but did he truly love him as a son? Or did he only love him as heir to his affairs?

And even more so, the thought that struck Erec like a knife in his chest: if being King meant compromising one's word, one's honor, for the sake of the masses, was that something Erec could do? Erec had lived his entire life for honor, and he would give up his life for honor, no matter what the cost. But as King, could he afford that luxury? He would destroy himself for the sake of honor—but could he destroy a kingdom?

# CHAPTER TWENTY-ONE

Gwendolyn stood at the head of the huge ship, leading her fleet, peering out into the horizon and rising up and down as the ship was buoyed on the rolling waves. She breathed deep, knowing that every moment, every spray of an ocean wave, took them further and further from the Ring.

They sailed into a driving wind and mist, the rain finally pausing, but the thick, gloomy clouds refusing to recede. Despite the summer, it was getting colder the further north they went, and Gwen pulled her cloak tight around her shoulders. She clutched Guwayne, holding him tight to her chest, relishing his warmth, rocking him as she looked out and wondered of the future that lay ahead of them.

Gwendolyn did not turn around and look back—not once—even though she knew that the mainland of the Ring was now far from sight. She feared that, if she turned around, she would spot Romulus's dragons, that somehow they would break through Argon's shield and pursue them. Recalling their awful sight, the heat of their flames as they'd approached, she shuddered; she did not want to jinx it.

All around her, all there was, was ocean, water in every direction, an endless monotony. But it didn't matter; she welcomed water for a change. She couldn't bear to look back behind her, in the direction where her home once stood. It was too painful. Everything, she knew, that she ever loved and cherished was now burned to the ground; King's Court, she felt sick to think, was now being enjoyed by Romulus and his soldiers, by his dragons. All of her people throughout the Ring, the ones who had not had time to evacuate with her, were surely dead. Her homeland was no more. Gwen felt gutted; she felt as if somehow it were all her fault. She wished dearly that she could have rescued more of her people.

All that remained, all the hope she had left in the world, lay straight ahead. She looked about and saw her dozens of ships and could not help but feel that they were stealing away like exiles, a mass exodus from the bounties of the Ring to the lonely, craggy, stormy Upper Isles. Gwen trembled to think that the rest of her days, her people's days, would be doomed to such a place; but at least, she told herself, they were alive. They had survived. And for now, that was all that mattered.

Gwen knew there would be no welcoming party waiting to greet her; only a cold, if not hostile, reception by Tirus's men. The last she'd heard, she'd dispatched Reece to apologize to Tirus; who knew how Tirus had taken it. Would he be gracious upon their arrival? she wondered. Somehow, she doubted it. She now inhabited a cold, barren place, stuck between one adversary and the next, she and all her people forced to fight, one way or the other, in whatever direction they chose, just to survive.

Gwen closed her eyes and tried to push out the horror; she thought of all the people she'd had to leave behind, spread throughout the Ring, all under her care. She shook her head, thinking of all the families who must be dead right now, eviscerated by Romulus's hand and the breath of his dragons. She did not understand how it could have happened. Romulus, somehow, had managed to lower the Shield, and had managed to somehow control all those dragons. She had sensed doom coming, yet she'd never imagined such breadth of destruction.

Gwen felt like collapsing, like giving up, so weak and tired and drained in every possible way, but she forced herself to be strong. After all, she was Queen, and she still ruled, and her people were looking to her. Her queendom had shrunk to this ship, this fleet, these hundreds of people, yet still, it was something. She had to go on for their sake.

Gwen craved someone to talk to, now more than ever. She thought of Argon, and recalled how Ralibar had caught up to them, had deposited Argon's limp body, unmoving, on the deck, where he still lay; Gwendolyn and the others had tried to awaken him, to no avail. Her heart had broken at the sight, and she wondered if Argon had left them this time for good. Ralibar had taken off, she did not know where, and she did not know if he would ever come back to her, either. Gwendolyn felt more alone than ever. Without Argon, without

131

Ralibar, without Thor—and with only these few thousand men—what hope did any of them have? They would be lucky, she knew, to even reach the Upper Isles. If Argon's shield lowered, they would be finished. They could not withstand a direct attack from Romulus and his dragons, and she knew that eventually, they would surely follow them.

Gwen looked out to the horizon, to the stormy seas, and wished that now, more than ever, Thorgrin was here, by her side.

"My Queen?" came a soft voice.

Gwendolyn turned to see her brother, Kendrick, come up beside her, along with her other brother, Godfrey, and Steffen and Aberthol. She took comfort in their presence, and was grateful that at least they had survived.

"We won't be approaching the Isles for some time, if even today. Night looms, and the wind is picking up. Will you come below with the rest of us? Standing up here will make you sick, and will not make us arrive any faster."

Gwendolyn shook her head.

"I don't want us to arrive any faster. I want to return to the Ring. But it is gone. Destroyed forever," she replied, despondent. "And it is my fault."

She turned and faced them, and Kendrick and the others exchanged a grave look. Gwen told herself to be strong.

"It is not your fault, my lady," Steffen replied. "On the contrary, you saved all these people you see here."

"I expect us to arrive at daybreak," Kendrick said, "and our men will need to be prepared. I doubt we shall find a warm reception. We intercepted a raven heading for the Ring. It brings news that our brother has killed Tirus."

"What!?" Gwen said, shocked.

Kendrick nodded, gravely.

"I sent him to apologize and he murdered the man?" Gwen asked, trying to process it. She could hardly conceive what had happened, and she was furious at Reece.

"Word is that there is an open revolt on the island, that our men are cut off, stuck on their small fleet of ships. Perhaps we can reach them in time."

Gwendolyn nodded, determined.

"Tirus deserved to die," she said, "yet Reece was foolish to defy my orders. That said, we abandon no one. We will sail as hard as we can throughout the night, and if need be, we shall fight to the death to rescue our men."

She looked to her men, who all looked to her for leadership, and her voice rose with confidence.

"Do not worry," she told them. "We shall take back the Upper Isles. At least in this we shall be successful. And once there, we shall establish a new stronghold, a new home for us, expatriates of the Ring."

They all nodded, and she could see that they took some reassurance in her words, in her confidence.

"And what if Argon's spell should falter?" Godfrey asked. "What if those dragons should be let loose? How can we possibly fight them off?"

"Romulus now has the Ring," Gwen replied. "Perhaps he shall be content with that and not pursue us."

"And if he is not?" Aberthol pressed.

"Then we shall have no choice but to fight him. And his dragons."

The men looked grave.

"But my queen, we cannot win," Aberthol said. "It would be us against a host of dragons—and a million-man army."

Gwendolyn nodded, realizing he was correct.

"For now, let us reach the Isles, free our brothers, and establish a home. Let us pray that Argon's shield holds."

"And if not?" Aberthol pressed. "Have we no other options?"

Gwen turned and looked out to the horizon, as somber as her mood, knowing they did not.

"Yes," she said. "We can do what we always do: fight for our honor—and fight to the death."

*

Godfrey and Illepra sat below deck as night fell, the huge ship rocking up and down. Godfrey leaned his back against the wall as Illepra tended his wounds, wrapping a bandage around his arm again and again. As he studied her, so close, he noticed a difference in how she looked at him. Before, she'd always looked at him in a disapproving matter—and yet now, he was surprised to see her smiling at him, wrapping his arm slowly and affectionately, cutting the bandage tenderly, tending his wounds with love and affection.

"You've changed," she said to him.

Godfrey looked at her, puzzled.

"How so?" he asked. "That's funny, because I was just thinking the same thing about you."

"You're not the boy you once were," she said. "You are a man now. You stood up and fought as a man. You risked your life for others, for the sake of our city, as few others would. I'm surprised. I would not have expected it from you."

Godfrey blushed, looking away.

"I did not do it in order for you to be proud. I was not seeking your approval, or anyone else's—especially not my dead father's. I did it for myself. And for my sister."

"Yet nonetheless, you did it. I know you are not your father. But I'll tell you something: I think you are going to become even greater than your father ever was."

Godfrey raised his brow, surprised at her words.

"You mock me," he said.

She shook her head, and her face grew serious.

"Your father was born into rank and privilege," she said. "He was born to be a king. You, on the other hand, had nothing expected of you, being the middle child. You came to it on your own. You did not accept the status quo, but rather you sought out for yourself the best way to live, and you came to your conclusions in your own right. Not because anyone forced you to. Not because anyone expected anything of you. You were going on one track, and you turned it around, all by yourself. You transcended who you were. It is easy to become a

134

warrior when being a warrior is all that one's ever done; it is much harder, though, when one comes to it later in life, when one decides on one's own that he can be a warrior, too, just like anybody else."

Godfrey felt touched by her words as he processed them; it was the first time in his life that anyone had ever showered him with praise. He blushed.

"There are many warriors who can wield a sword and spear better than I," he said humbly. "I shall never be able to match their skill, not this late in life."

Illepra shook her head.

"That is not the point, and that alone is not what makes a warrior," she said. "It takes honor. Will. Sacrifice. And that is what you now have. Whether you see it in yourself or not, I see it in you."

Illepra surprised Godfrey as she suddenly leaned in and kissed him on the lips. He did not resist.

And then, after a stunned moment, he kissed her back.

They held the kiss for a long time, until finally, Illepra pulled back, smiling at him.

"It's been a long time since I kissed anyone," she said.

"Then we must do it again," Godfrey said with a smile, and he leaned in and kissed her again. As they held the kiss, their warm lips meeting on this cold night, Godfrey soon forgot all about the pain in his arm. For the first time in as long as he could remember, on this rocking ship in the middle of nowhere, he felt at home in the world.

Maybe, he thought, this warrior thing was not so bad after all.

*

Steffen stood on the deck of the ship in the rain and wind as the gloom gave way to twilight, standing not far from Gwendolyn. He stood just far enough away to give her privacy as she stood looking out at the sea, as if looking for some long-lost friend, clutching Guwayne. He had remained up here long after the others had gone below, unable to part from her, to leave her here all by herself.

Beside him stood Arliss, who had stayed by his side for most of the trip, as she had ever since they'd met. Steffen was flattered that she cared about him; he had never experienced anything like it before, and he was overwhelmed with love for her.

"She wants to be alone," Arliss said to Steffen. "We should go down below, with the others." Her voice was filled with caring and concern for him.

It was such a foreign feeling for Steffen to have anyone care about him; he kept doubting whether Arliss really loved him, or whether she was just playing a cruel trick on him, just pretending to love him—like everyone else in his life had.

But the more time Steffen had spent with her, the more sincere he could feel she was. She really loved him. It was a hard feeling for him to accept. No one in his life had ever, truly, unconditionally loved him for exactly who he was. He almost didn't know how to react. All that he knew was that he felt an overwhelming rush of love and gratitude for her.

"Please go below, my love," he said to her. "You will get cold and wet up here, too. I myself cannot go below. Not with Gwendolyn above."

"But she urged you to go below."

He shrugged.

"I don't like having her out of my sight. At least not when Thorgrin is not here. I owe her a great debt."

Arliss nodded.

"I understand. Our Queen is most endearing; she has taken me in like a sister, and I feel the same loyalty to her as you do. But no danger could befall her here. She is amongst her own people. On a ship, in the middle of an ocean."

"I know," Steffen said. "But it is my duty. And my duty I take very seriously."

Arliss clutched the rail, looking out to sea, and Steffen detected sadness in her face.

"What is it, my love?" Steffen asked.

She sighed.

"When I think of the Ring, of all we've left behind, it is overwhelming. It is hard to conceive. Everyone we've known and

136

loved, everything, completely destroyed. The Ring is now a wasteland. How can it be?"

Steffen shook his head, understanding, feeling hollow out himself. There was nothing he could say. He thought back to his hometown, to all his family, now surely dead, and while they were never kind to him, still he felt sadness.

"Isn't it hard for you to think of?" she pressed. "That life will never be the same? That that we can never return home?"

Steffen looked out to the horizon and sighed.

"For me, I've nothing left behind," he said. "Everything we left back home, all those towns of the Ring, they hold nothing for me. As for the people I care about, they are here. We can reinvent our hometown. It is a chance to start life over again. All that I care about in this world is my duty. Which means Gwendolyn. And now, of course, you," he said as he lowered his head and blushed.

Arliss, clearly touched, looked at him and smiled, then kissed him.

They held the kiss for a long time.

She sighed as she looked out to sea.

"The people we grew up with were cruel," she said. "They do not deserve our tears. Yet still, a part of me feels guilty. After all, we're the only ones that escaped. What if I hadn't come to King's Court? What if I had never met you? I would be dead right now."

Steffen gazed out at the horizon and realized he hadn't thought of that.

"I love you," she said. "I owe you my life."

Steffen shook his head.

"You owe me nothing. I did not save you. The fates did."

"But the fates brought you to me."

She leaned in close, and Steffen put his arm around her shoulder, holding her tight, rubbing her shoulder which was trembling. It was an amazing feeling, to hold a girl tight, to feel wanted, loved. He felt as if his life mattered more than it had before, and he felt less alone in the world.

"My love, you're trembling," he said. "The mist thickens. Please. Go down below."

"Only if you promise to join me."

Needing her to go below, finally, he nodded.

"I will," he said. "Soon enough."

Arliss leaned in, gave him a kiss, and quickly descended below deck.

Steffen turned back to Gwendolyn. She was still standing there, alone, her back to him, gazing out at the ocean, holding Guwayne. He wondered what thoughts were racing through her mind.

Steffen could not let her stand here like this, all alone, freezing cold. He resolved to go to her once again, and to implore her to come below. He knew she would not, proud and stubborn as she was, and with so much on her mind. She felt as if she had to stay up here, he knew, to sacrifice herself for her people; she always had. Steffen loved and admired her for that. But he wanted her safe.

As Steffen began to approach her, he suddenly spotted motion out of the corner of his eye. Something moved quickly in the darkness, on the other side of the deck, and his heart leapt as he saw a figure wearing a black hood. He was sprinting in the gloom and fog, heading along the side of the ship—and running right for Gwendolyn.

Steffen saw a gleam in the light, and he realized, with dread, what it was: a dagger. The man, he realized, was an assassin, a blade shining in his hands, on his way to kill Gwendolyn.

"Gwendolyn!" Steffen shouted.

Steffen broke into a run, sprinting for her—but he realized the assassin already had a wide lead on him.

Gwen turned at his shout, and as she did, she saw the assassin racing for her. She clutched Guwayne tight, then she waited until the last moment and dodged the knife; the assassin charged past her, just missing, his knife cutting through the air as he stumbled across the bow.

That was all the time Steffen needed. He raced forward as the assassin circled around, and without hesitating, he drew his sword and plunged it through the assassin's heart.

The man cried out, gasping, blood gurgling from his mouth and throat, and collapsed in Steffen's arms, as if hugging him. Steffen dropped him, and the man collapsed to the deck, dead.

Alarm horns sounded on deck, and within moments, dozens of knights, led by Kendrick and Godfrey, came rushing out of the bowels of the ship, racing toward Gwendolyn, who stood there, ashen.

"Are you okay?" Kendrick asked her, breathing hard. He looked down at the dead body in horror, then looked in every direction for any signs of another attacker. But there were none.

Gwendolyn nodded.

Kendrick reached down and pulled the dead assassin to his feet. He yanked back his hood and examined his face with disgust.

"One of Tirus's men," Godfrey said, stepping forward. "A spy."

Kendrick picked him up high overhead and hurled him over the side of the ship. They watched as his body splashed in the ocean and was quickly carried away by the waves.

"Steffen saved my life," Gwen said.

All eyes turned to Steffen, and he blushed from the attention, looking down.

"You are a true soldier," Kendrick said to him, placing a grateful hand on his shoulder. "Our family owes you a great debt."

Gwendolyn faced him.

"I owe you my life, once again," she said. "And this time, my baby's life, too. You are more than a servant. From this day forward, you are a knight."

Steffen flushed in shock.

"Kneel," she said.

He did so, and she took Kendrick's sword and touched the tip to each of his shoulders.

"And rise, Sir Steffen," she said.

Steffen rose slowly, as the men all around him let out an approving cheer, each rushing forward to clap him on the back. The world felt like it was spinning around him; he had never anticipated anything like this in his lifetime.

The storm picked up, and Steffen joined the others as they all, including Gwendolyn, went below deck, and as he went, he took one long last look out to the raging oceans, and wondered what other dangers this trek would have in store for them.

## CHAPTER TWENTY-TWO

Thor lay in the mud on his back, looking up at Andronicus, who raised a battle-ax high with both hands and prepared to split him in two.

Thor sensed his father's hatred for him, his rage, felt that he was about to be destroyed—and worst of all, he knew this was all his own creation. He knew that everything he saw before him was but a reflection of his own consciousness, and yet he could not turn it off. He would die here, in this place, and all because of his own subconscious, his own worst fears.

Thor closed his eyes and forced himself to summon his inner power. He summoned all of his training sessions with Argon, heard Argon's words ringing through his ears.

*You're stronger than any evil in the universe. You and the universe are not separate. Do not resist the energy around you. And most of all, do not resist yourself.*

So many times Thor had heard Argon's words, had tried to contemplate their meaning, had trained and tried to put them into action. Sometimes he had been successful, and other times not. Thor had never gained perfect mastery over his powers, over the universe. As he focused, went into his deepest depths, Thor realized that there was always something inside him holding him back; he had never fully embraced his powers. He had never truly embraced who he was. Always, he'd seen his powers as separate from himself. Now, for the first time, he realized that he and his powers were one. They were tied to the very fabric of his being.

Thor felt a surge of strength as he realized that he was proud to embrace his powers, proud of who he was.

Thor opened his eyes to see the ax coming down for him—but this time, it was different. This time, he saw it all in slow motion; this time he was a part of it, not separate from it. And as it came down,

140

Thor suddenly felt complete control of his mind. He rolled out of the way, and at the same time, he turned the mud beside him into water; Andronicus's ax came plunging down, just missing him, instead disappearing into a puddle of water.

Andronicus stumbled forward as the ax plunged in, and he fell face first into the mud.

Thor rolled to his feet on the muddy landscape, and his intuition took over. Instead of searching for a weapon, instead of combing the landscape, Thor felt that he could change the landscape to suit him. He could control it.

Thor turned and his eyes locked on the Destiny Sword, still embedded in the mud. As Andronicus regained his feet, Thor walked casually over to the sword, gently laid both hands on the hilt, and closed his eyes. He felt the power of it throbbing, coursing through his veins.

*I shall wield this sword. I shall wield it because I and the sword are not separate. I and the sword are one.*

Thor, eyes closed, heard the distinct sound of metal, felt the vibration in his hand, and he looked up to see himself holding the blade high overhead, sparkling above him. His old friend was back in his hand.

Andronicus charged and swung with his ax, and Thorgrin calmly stepped forward and slashed, cutting Andronicus's ax in half by the staff. The ax head detached and went flying into the mud, as Andronicus swung harmlessly with the other half of it.

Andronicus stumbled past Thor, then regained his balance and turned and faced him. This time, Andronicus faced Thor with dread, fear in his eyes, as he looked at Thor wielding the Destiny Sword. Thor felt more powerful than he'd ever had. He felt he finally had complete control over his surroundings.

"You are my father," Thor said. "But that does not mean that I am your son. We choose our fathers. We have the power to choose. And I do not choose you."

Thor charged and let out a great battle cry as he brought his Destiny Sword down for Andronicus, determined to wipe him out once and for all. Andronicus raised his shaft in defense, and Thor sliced it in half, the blade continuing down and slicing Andronicus's chest, drawing blood.

Andronicus cried out in pain from the wound and stumbled, landing on his back.

As Andronicus lay there, bleeding, Thor stood over him, wielding the sword. Andronicus looked up at him as Thor raised the sword to finish him off.

Suddenly, though, the view before Thor changed, and for the first time, Thor felt uncertain. Andronicus changed before Thor's eyes. He began to shrink, and his grotesque body and face changed to one that was very human.

By the time the transformation was finished, Andronicus was a regular man, a proud and noble warrior, wearing the royal uniform and crest of the MacGils. The elder brother of King MacGil. He resembled King MacGil, and he looked uncannily like Thor.

Andronicus raised a hand to Thorgrin.

"Here I am," he said. "You are seeing me. I am the man that was once your father, before I changed. I am the man who your mother met and fell in love with. It is I, your original father. Save me, Thorgrin. Save me for all time."

Thor hesitated. He felt something was wrong, and yet he could not let his father just lay there, wounded. So Thor reached down, grasped his hand, and pulled him to his feet.

As he did, his father grasped his arm so hard it hurt, and he would not let go. Thor tried to free himself, but he could not. Andronicus smiled, raised a dagger hidden in his belt, and stabbed Thor in the chest.

Thor gasped as the blade pierced him, feeling pain beyond what he had ever felt. He had been tricked, and he realized that he was dying.

As Thor felt his world ebbing away, light-headed, weak, he forced himself to focus. He knew that he could stop this. He knew he had the power to transcend the physical plane, to find another way. This land was forcing him to become greater than himself, to use powers he never had before.

Thor closed his eyes and summoned the universe to extract the blade from his chest.

Suddenly the dagger popped out, and Andronicus stepped back, holding it, looking shocked. Thor used the energy of the air to heal his wound, to stop the blood. As he closed his eyes he placed his palms over his chest, his hands glowing with unreal power and heat, and as he moved them away, his wound was completely healed.

Andronicus stared back, open-mouthed in shock.

Thor raised the Destiny Sword once again, and this time, he stuck it in the ground beside him, letting it go. For the first time, he realized he did not need it. He was more sorcerer than human. He was a Druid after all. He had the power of the entire universe at his fingertips, and that was more powerful than any piece of steel.

"I don't need a sword to kill you, Father. I need only the power of my mind. You exist in the deepest levels of my mind. Aside from that, you're powerless."

Thor then aimed a single palm at his father, and as he did, a ball of light shot through it, engulfing him. Andronicus shouted as he flew backwards through the air, the shout fading as he went farther and farther away, at the speed of light, flying to the horizon, before he finally disappeared completely.

As Thor stood there in the stillness, suddenly the fog all around him lifted. The skies opened up, the sun came through, and slowly, the landscape before him transformed. The mud transformed into grass, bright, shiny, vibrant grass, the dead trees blossomed, and birds arrived, singing. Winter turned to summer, desolation to bounty.

As Thor looked to the horizon, he no longer saw emptiness. Instead, he saw, in the distance, a castle, perched on the edge of a cliff, a great walkway leading to it.

He felt his heart pounding as he recognized the place of his dreams as he knew, he just knew, that his mother lay on the road before him.

# CHAPTER TWENTY-THREE

Alistair walked side-by-side with Erec's mother, their arms locked, Erec's mother smiling as they wound their way along the copper-lined walkways on the edge of the cliffs. Alistair had been overcome by how kind his mother had been to him, so gracious, taking her in as if she were her own daughter. Alistair had never met her mother, and had always wanted a mother in her life—and in the short time she'd spent with Erec's mom, she already realized how great it could be. A part of her felt complete that had not before.

As they walked, a dozen attendants following them, fanning the Queen, they reached the edge of a plateau, demarcated by a high copper railing, and Alistair looked out, awestruck at the view. It was as if the whole world were spread out below them. In the valleys below Alistair saw thousands of dwellings, most shining with copper roofs, like a thousand points of light reflecting the sun. The islands were so fertile, despite their mountainous terrain, vineyards planted on cliffs, on hills, orchards of overripe fruit blossoming everywhere, adding color to the skyline, clinging to life on the steep terrain. The smell of their pungent flowers hung heavy in the air.

"It is one of the high points of the island," Erec's mother said softly beside her, looking out herself. "From up here you can see the entire capital, and even the villages hugging the shoreline. You can also see parts of the Tatrazen, where the great fog lingers in the valley."

Alistair followed her finger and saw, down below, beautiful villages built along the shoreline, hovering over the white sands, green and blue waters crashing against them. A mist hung over the islands, and the air was the freshest she'd ever breathed, filled with the smell of ocean and orange blossoms. The sun shone so strongly here, she felt its caress, its rays warming her whole body.

Alistair felt tucked in here, deeply at rest in this place. She was surprised. She had expected to feel disoriented in the new terrain, to miss the Ring; yet for some reason, here in the Southern Isles she felt more at home than she'd ever had.

"Your island is beautiful," Alistair said. "Thank you for your graciousness."

Erec's mother smiled wide and wrapped an arm around Alistair's shoulder, hugging her.

"You are Erec's beloved," she said, "which means you are a daughter to me. I will always love you, as he loves you. You can come to me with anything."

Alistair smiled, feeling so good to be embraced by a mother for the first time in her life. She felt loved here, and her love for Erec, if possible, felt even stronger.

"Are you ready for the sacred water?" she asked.

Alistair looked at her, puzzled.

"What is that?" she asked.

Her mother pointed.

Alistair turned and saw, near the edge of the cliff, a wide hole in the smooth marble, in which was a bubbling spring, steam rising from it. Inside it sat Erec's sister, Dauphine, her back to them, her head resting against the stone and her arms spread out as she looked out over the endless vistas of the island.

"It is the custom of the women here to immerse themselves weekly in the waters. They are very relaxing, and they are said to have purifying elements. A bride will always immerse herself the day before her wedding. It is said to bring good luck."

Alistair looked at her, wide-eyed, wondering if she heard correctly.

His mother nodded back.

"That's right. Tomorrow you will be wed."

Alistair's heart suddenly started to pound.

"*Tomorrow!?*" Alistair said, flummoxed. "But I haven't even had time to...I haven't even prepared..."

His mother smiled and held out a hand.

"Do not worry," she said. "Your dresses have been prepared. There is a wide selection for you to choose from, as well as the finest

145

royal jewels in our vault. Our people have been preparing for this for moons. It will be the most spectacular wedding you've ever seen."

Alistair was flabbergasted. On the one hand, she was delighted to actually be getting married to Erec; but then again, she had no idea this was coming so soon, and she hadn't even had time to mentally prepare for the biggest day of her life.

"But why so sudden?" Alistair asked. "Shouldn't I have helped to prepare?"

Erec's mother shook her head.

"We here on the Southern Islands have superstitions around weddings. We believe they must take place immediately. It is our custom that when a bride is proposed to, she is wed immediately. We are a people that does not delay, that follows through instantly with what we pledge. It is one of many customs and peculiarities you'll come to learn about us. I hope it does not offend you?"

Alistair smiled wide as she thought it all over. They were indeed an unusual people, yet she didn't mind their customs; she thought they were quirky, and she liked them. And the idea of getting married to Erec immediately filled her heart with love. She was also so grateful to them for all the preparation they had taken.

Alistair shook her head.

"On the contrary," she replied. "I will be delighted to marry your son. Even if it took place at this very moment."

His mother smiled back, and she turned and began to lead Alistair over to the hot springs.

"Dauphine," his mother called out sharply, a harshness to her tone that Alistair had not expected. "Turn to us. Rise and greet your sister-in-law."

Dauphine scoffed, keeping her back to them, still ignoring them.

"Dauphine, did you hear me?" his mother pressed.

Gradually, Dauphine rose from the waters. She was entirely naked, and she stood and turned, facing them, expressionless. Alistair blushed and looked away. Dauphine stood there and stared her down coldly.

146

"Consider yourself greeted," she said, and then she turned and sat back down in the water.

Alistair wondered, once again, what Dauphine's problems were; she seemed like a troubled person. Either that, or she just truly hated Alistair.

Attendants rushed forward and helped the Queen and Alistair undress, giving them robes as they led them to the springs.

As Alistair stepped down the stone steps into the hot water, it felt so good, the warm water bubbling all over her, filled with a lotion she did not recognize, soaking into her muscles, making her feel completely relaxed. Alistair looked out over the endless landscape, perched as they were at the edge of a cliff, the soft breezes caressing her, and she felt as if she were floating in heaven.

"Dauphine," her mother said, "be gracious to our new guest. In but hours, she will be your Queen."

"She will *not* be my Queen," Dauphine said, forceful.

"She will," his mother insisted. "She is Erec's bride. If you have any love for him, you will be gracious to her."

Dauphine closed her eyes and shook her head.

Alistair sat there, feeling uncomfortable, feeling as if she were the cause of all this upset, her relaxation disappearing.

"You disgrace your family to treat her so rudely," his mother pressed. "And you should not be sitting in the center chair. That is reserved for the bride."

Dauphine opened her eyes, stormy, and glared at her mother.

"She has a tongue. She can speak for herself."

Alistair blushed, not wanting to be caught between the two of them, not a confrontational person. Alistair realized how much Dauphine hated her and she did not understand why.

"You may sit wherever you choose," Alistair said. "I wish no special seat for myself."

"There, Mother. We have spoken," Dauphine snapped. "Is that enough for you?"

His mother shook her head, fuming.

"Your father would be ashamed of you."

147

Dauphine sighed, stood abruptly, and stormed out of the hot springs, the water splashing. She hurried up the steps, naked, brushing off the robe the attendants wanted to give her, and stormed away from the plateau.

"Dauphine, get back here!" her mother called.

But she quickly disappeared from view.

His mother blushed as she looked at Alistair.

"Please forgive her rudeness. It is not indicative of our people. I'm afraid I did not raise her as harshly as I should have."

Alistair shook her head.

"Please, don't apologize."

"It is just that she is very attached to Erec. She always has been. And she hasn't seen him in so many years."

"Please, don't apologize for her. You have been a most gracious host, and I am honored to have you as a mother-in-law."

His mother smiled, sadly, and then the two sat back and closed their eyes.

Suddenly, just as Alistair was beginning to relax in the silence, all throughout the land there came the sound of bells tolling. This was followed by a huge cheer below.

The noise rose, louder and louder, and Alistair opened her eyes in alarm.

"What is happening?" she asked, wondering how many more strange customs these people had. It sounded like a great celebration.

Erec's mother opened her eyes and smiled wide. She laughed and held up her hands to the sky.

"Those are death bells," she explained. "My husband, he is dead!"

She laughed and laughed, clearly filled with delight.

Alistair looked at her, uncomprehending.

"Then why is everyone celebrating?" she asked. "Why are you smiling?"

His mother sighed and looked at her.

"In the Southern Isles, death is not something to be mourned. It is to be celebrated. We are forbidden to mourn death here. Instead, we

148

celebrate the life. In fact, for us, it is the greatest cause of all to celebrate."

The bells tolled and tolled, and as the cheers rose to a fever pitch, Alistair realized how foreign this place was, and how much indeed she had left to learn about this nation.

## CHAPTER TWENTY-FOUR

Thor stood before the skywalk, holding his breath as a cold gust of wind smacked him in the face. In the distance, at the other end of the walk, he saw great cliffs rising up into the sky, and perched on the edge, an ancient castle, its doors gleaming gold.

His mother's castle.

The wind howled as he stood there, regarding the sight, this view from his dreams, with a mix of anticipation and worry. The skywalk was narrow, slick with the ocean spray and a hanging mist, and beneath it, the fall to the raging ocean and cliffs below was several hundred feet. It was a death fall.

Thor looked out at the vista with a sense of wonder. There was magic in the air here, he could feel it. This entire world felt surreal; it was the landscape of his dreams, come to life, dreams that had haunted him all his life. And now it was real.

Or was it real? Was this all just another creation of his mind?

Thor could no longer be sure. But this felt more real to him anything he had seen. Certainly more real than one of his dreams. And now that he was here, inside his dream, he wasn't sure how it would end.

Thor knew that his mother was there, on the other side of that skywalk, in that castle; he could sense it. He felt himself trembling, excited beyond belief to finally lay eyes on her—and nervous. What would she look like? Would she be kind and loving to him, as she had been in his dreams? Would she be happy to see him?

And then there was the worst thought of all, the one that Thor was afraid to entertain: what if she was not there at all?

Thor knew that standing here, waiting, would do him no good. The time had come.

Thor braced himself and took his first step onto the walkway; as he did, the wind howled. He stumbled immediately on the slick ground, then regained his balance. He took several more steps, cautious.

The sound of the waves grew louder, and Thor looked down and saw them, smashing against the rocks, the mist rising up into the air, carried by the wind. He took another step, then another, and as he did, he could not help but feel as if he were leaving one world behind and entering a new one. He felt as if he were walking into the very depths of his subconscious.

Thor gained momentum, walking faster and faster, and soon he was halfway across. He knew it could not be this easy. He began to wonder what other tests might lay before him, what else his subconscious might create.

He had barely thought it, when there appeared before him a lone figure. Thor blinked several times before he realized it was his adopted father, the man who had raised him back in his home village, the man who had been so cruel to him. Behind him there suddenly appeared, too, Thor's three adopted brothers.

Thor realized his mind was bringing him back to his childhood, to his earliest days, creating another obstacle for him. It was creating, he realized, all the people in his life who had always tried to keep him down, the final obstacles to his getting where he wanted to go.

"You will come no further," said his adopted father. "You are not worthy. And only the worthy can cross here."

"Who are you to tell me I'm not worthy?" Thor replied, finally standing up to this man, as he had not done his entire life. Thor's inability to stand up for himself, to express himself, to tell this father figure how he'd really felt, had been one of his main sources of disappointment his entire life. Now, finally, he was mustering the courage.

Thor's three brothers scowled behind him while Thor's father stood there, hands on hips, defiant.

"If you think you can cross here, Thorgrin, you will have to get past me."

His father charged, and he was faster than Thor realized. Thor reached to grab the Destiny Sword, and was horrified to see it was gone.

Thor, defenseless against his father's charge and reacting too late, found himself tackled by him, driven down to the ground. The two of them went sliding along the narrow skywalk.

Thor slid right for the edge, when he suddenly spun around and threw his father over, wrestling him, the two of them rolling back and forth as they slid.

Thor finally landed on top of his father, pinning him to the ground, choking him, as his father choked Thor back. Thor heard his three brothers charging towards him, heard each draw their swords, each about to stab Thor in the back.

Thor closed his eyes.

*You are not real. You do not really exist. You are my subconscious. You are my doubts and fears. Everything I see around me, everything in the world, is me. It is I giving you power. And now, I will stop giving you that power.*

Thor summoned the deepest part of himself to force himself to become stronger, to fight without fighting, to wage war without weapons. It was time, he realized, to make his mind stronger than his body.

Thor felt a wave of heat rush over him, felt his world turn a blinding white, and as he opened his eyes, he found himself grabbing not his father's neck, but the dirt on the walkway beneath him. His father had vanished.

Thor turned, and saw his brothers were gone, too. All that was left was the howling of the wind, and waves of mist, rolling in.

Thor breathed out, relieved, then slowly regained his feet. He continued walking along the skywalk, chiding himself to keep his mind strong. He was becoming, he knew, his own worst enemy. This entire trek across the Land of the Druids had been one long quest to master his mind and that, he was beginning to realize, was the hardest battle of all. Thor would rather face an entire army alone. His mind could take him to the deepest and darkest places unexpectedly, and he still did not have the control he needed to prevent it from going there.

How did one gain that control? he wondered. It was a struggle, he realized, that he would have to continue to train to master.

As Thor walked, the gusts of wind knocking him off balance, he decided he could use the power of his mind to lessen the power of the wind. He was starting to see how he was one with nature, the universe, with everything around him. The wind calmed, and he stood straighter, walked more proudly, had better balance as he continued along the walkway. He felt the universe converging all around him, his footing getting more sure.

Thor was amazed to realize that he was approaching the end of the skywalk. When he was just feet away from the end, from the cliff on which his mother's castle stood, suddenly, one more figure stood before him, blocking the way.

Thor blinked several times, trying to process who he saw before him. It made no sense. Facing him was a formidable foe, wearing armor unlike any other Thor had seen.

Standing there, facing him, was *him*.

Thorgrin.

Thor stared back at the exact replica of himself, a fierce and formidable warrior, who stood there, braced for battle, holding the Destiny Sword at his side. He examined this warrior and tried to understand if he was real, or just another creation of his mind. How could there be another one of him in the universe?

"Why do you block me from my mother's entrance?" Thor asked.

"Because you are not worthy," came the reply.

"Not worthy to meet my own mother?" Thor asked.

The warrior stared back, expressionless, unflinching.

"This is a castle for the initiated," he replied. "Only the most powerful can enter. I am the guardian. You will have to come through me."

Thor stared back, puzzled.

"But you are myself," Thor said.

"It is yourself you have not yet conquered," came the reply.

The warrior suddenly charged, raising the Destiny Sword high and bringing it down for Thor's head.

Thor felt something in his palm, and he looked down with joy to realize that he, too, was wielding the same Destiny Sword.

Thor raised it high and charged himself.

The two swords met in the middle, perfectly matched, sparks flying everywhere. Thor attacked, swinging left and right, and the warrior mimicked every exact blow, move for move. Whatever Thor did, the warrior did exactly, and Thor realized quickly that it was futile; there was no way he could win. This warrior knew what he knew. He anticipated his moves, and there was no way to defeat him.

Back and forth they went, Thor breathing hard, his arms and shoulders growing tired, until suddenly, as Thor slashed, the warrior did something Thor did not expect: he leaned back and kicked Thor in the chest.

Thor went flying, sliding on his back, along the walkway, all the way to the edge. He continued sliding on his slick armor, unable to stop himself, fearing he would slide off the edge.

Thor panicked as he slid over the edge, and began to fall.

Suddenly, the warrior was there, grabbing Thor's ankle, holding him by one hand, preventing him from falling. Thor looked down over his shoulder and saw the raging ocean below. He then looked up and saw has reflection staring down, as if debating whether or not to help him.

"Help me," Thor said, reaching up for him, upside down.

"And why should I?"

"I must see my mother," Thorgrin said. "I have not come all this way to die so close."

"And yet you lost in battle," the warrior said.

"But I lost to myself."

He shook his head.

"I am sorry," the warrior said. "You are still not strong enough."

Suddenly, the warrior let go.

Thor shrieked as he felt himself falling backwards, into the air, end over end, his screams echoing off the canyon as he plummeted towards the ocean, the rocks, and the sure death below.

# CHAPTER TWENTY-FIVE

The dawn broke unusually calm for the Upper Isles, as Reece, Stara, Matus, and Srog stood on board, facing east, watching the first sun creep over the horizon and greet the day. Behind them stood Commander Wolfson and his dozens of men, all on deck, all with weapons at the ready, all watching the horizon. The day was cold but surprisingly cloudless, the sky streaked with amber, and as the early morning darkness began to fade and the sun began to light the sky, Reece wondered what everyone else was surely wondering: when would the Upper Islanders attack?

The tension was so thick, Reece could feel it in the air. Now that dawn had broken, now that the stormy night was behind them, Reece was certain it was only a matter of time until Tirus's ships arrived from the open sea and flanked them from behind. They had decided to dig in, and Reece knew their cause would be a losing one. With a mere dozen ships left of Gwendolyn's fleet, there was no way they could defeat what would surely be dozens of ships, trapping them here in this harbor.

Reece examined the shoreline, and he saw the silhouettes of hundreds of Tirus's soldiers lined up, arrows at the ready, prepared to fire flame onto the fleet if they came into range. They were trapped.

Srog stepped forward, hands on his hips, looking out at the sky. He turned and looked back over his shoulder, at the open sea, at the direction from which Tirus's ships would surely approach.

"We must hold our position," Srog said. "And yet, at the same time, if we sit here we shall be killed."

Srog stood, thinking, and Reece stepped forward and surveyed the shores, thinking too. Reece knew Srog was right; he knew that something had to be done.

"What would your sister have us do?" Srog asked Reece.

Reece closed his eyes, thinking.

"She would not want us to wait and be killed," he answered. "She would want us to attack—just as my father would want us to attack. He always cherished the element of surprise. A smaller force attacking a bigger one: that is something they would not expect. If we are all to go down, we should go down boldly, attacking, with swords raised high. Not sitting here, waiting to be destroyed."

Reece opened his eyes and examined the shoreline.

"And since we can't sail out to sea, my father would want us to attack the shore."

Srog examined the shore, perplexed.

"But as we get into range, their arrows will set us all aflame," he protested.

Reece nodded.

"But if we move quickly enough, they cannot get all of us."

"And if we turn and sail out to sea?" Srog asked. "We could confront Tirus's fleet."

Matus stepped forward and shook his head.

"No," he said. "My brother's fleet dwarfs ours. They are well armed and well trained. It would be a slaughter."

"It seems it will be a slaughter either way," Srog observed.

Reece examined their options, staring, thinking hard. He came to a conclusion.

"Better to die on land than at sea," Reece said.

As they stood there, debating, suddenly a sailor high up on the mast called down urgently.

"My lord! They have arrived!"

All heads turned, and they rushed to the far side of the ship and looked out: the horizon was filled with the outline of ships, all sailing right for them. Tirus's fleet, on way to trap them in the harbor. To sandwich them between their ships and the shore.

Reece could feel the vice getting tighter.

Wolfson nodded, decided.

"Sail to the shore!" he commanded. "It is time to attack!"

*

156

Reece ducked as a flaming arrow sailed by his head, heart pounding as it just missed. All around him the boats filled with the panicked shouts of men, as their fleet sailed for shore, right into the army of flaming arrows flying for them. To speed up their attack, dozens of men rowed with all their might, trying to bring the ships faster to shore.

It was a slow, grueling effort, despite the crashing waves and current helping them toward land, and all around Reece, the air was punctuated by the screams of men, as flaming arrow after flaming arrow pierced them—and worse, began to pierce the sails and the wood.

Reece and the men scurried about, alternately rushing to put out the flames as fresh arrows landed, and firing back. Reece glanced out at the other ships, and he saw that some of them were on fire, the arrows having hit the sails too high, sending their ships into flame. Reece looked around with dread as he noticed that already several of their ships were flame, a flaming flotilla sailing into shore. Reece wondered how much of their fleet, if any, would even be left by the time they reached shores. If they ever did.

Reece turned and looked out at the sea, at their escape route, and spotted Tirus's fleet getting closer; he knew that they had to make shore. It was just a hundred yards—but they would be bloody.

Beside Reece, Stara fought bravely, not even ducking as she stood at the rail and fired off arrow after arrow at the shoreline, taking out men left and right. As a flaming arrow whizzed by Reece's head, he dropped his oar, stood, grabbed a bow, and joined her, firing back. He landed a perfect shot, from nearly a hundred yards, and he heard the cry of one of Tirus's men in the distance and watched him drop to the sand.

An arrow landed a few feet from Reece, lodging into a sail, and the flame began to spread on deck; Reece grabbed a pail of water and doused it immediately. It hissed and smoked and luckily he put it out—yet Reece did not know how many times they would be so lucky.

"Lower the sails!" the captain commanded.

Sailors rushed to execute his command, just as a flaming arrow hit one; they pulled faster and faster, Reece running over and joining them, and as the canvas lowered, Matus ran up and patted out the flames with his bare hand. He did it just in time, before the sail lit up entirely; leaving a large, black hole in its center.

Reece felt the speed of their ship drop, and Srog looked at the lowered sails with worry.

"It will cut out speed!" he yelled to the captain.

"I don't care!" the captain yelled back. "It's my ship! And we're not going down in flames!"

Reece, too, worried about the slower pace—and yet he realized it was a smart move, as the barrage of flaming arrows grew thicker and as more ships in their fleet began to catch fire. The sails just made them too vulnerable.

"LOWER THE SAILS! PASS IT ON!" the captain shouted out to the ship beside them, and their sailors yelled out his order to the next ship, and they to the next ship. One at a time, all the sails in his fleet began to lower. One of the ships could not lower them in time, and Reece flinched at the awful sound of his men shouting as they lit up in a great ball of flames.

As they got neared, now about seventy yards from shore, the currents were getting stronger, pulling them in amidst the crashing waves, and they regained their momentum. They passed the jetty on their right, and Reece spotted a group of soldiers, hidden amidst the rocks, suddenly rise and take aim for them.

Reece saw that Stara was in their line of fire, and that she had no idea, as she stood proudly and continued to fire for the shore; he turned and ran for her.

"Stara!" he cried.

Reece sprinted across the deck and dove, tackling her, driving her down to the deck. They hit the deck hard, Stara crying out as she impacted the wood. Yet as they sank, an arrow sailed by exactly where she had just been. The arrow pierced Reece's shoulder instead, and he shouted out in pain.

Reece lay there, groaning, looking at Stara, who looked at him, equally wide-eyed. Reece could tell by her expression that she realized he had just saved her life.

He wanted to talk to her, but he was in too much pain; the flaming arrow was still on fire in his shoulder, and Stara, horrified, patted it out. With each pat, it hurt Reece even more.

"Stay still!" she cried. "I have to get this out!"

Reece looked over, and saw the head was not all the way in, only a few inches. But still, it felt as if were piercing through his entire body.

"I don't know if you should—" he began.

But before he could finish the words, Stara reached down and yanked the arrow out with all her might.

Reece shrieked, blood gushing from the wound. It was the most painful thing he'd ever experienced; Stara quickly reached up with her palm and covered the blood. She then used her teeth to pull a strip of cloth from her shirt, and wrapped it around his shoulder several times. More arrows whizzed by overhead, and they both ducked low to miss them.

Reece looked down, his wound throbbing, and saw his bandage seeping blood. Stara tore another strip and tied it again.

"Sorry," Stara said, as Reece winced. "It's not exactly what I'd call a lady's touch."

There came a great shout and a commotion on board, and Reece looked up with surprise to see several of Tirus's men jumping on onboard as they sailed closer to shore, alongside the jetty of rocks. Reece looked up and saw they were now hardly thirty yards from shore, and Tirus's men were lined up, all leaping for the ship. Several bounced off the slick rails and landed, screaming, into the waters; others grabbed on but were knocked off by Reece's men. Yet enough of them managed to land on board, and to pull themselves up. They were invading the ship.

Reece scrambled to his feet, along with Stara, raised his sword with his good arm, and raced for the invaders. He stabbed two of them before they could get over the rail and sent them hurling back

159

into the waters. A third, though, landed beside him, and he raised his sword and swung around, aiming for Reece's exposed neck. Reece could not turn in time to block it, and he braced himself.

Stara lunged forward, wielding a long spear, and stabbed the soldier in the chest before he could complete his blow. The man cried as she jabbed him backwards, over the rail, over the ship, and tumbling backwards into the waters.

Reece looked at her, stunned, and so grateful.

"Looks like we're even," he said.

She smiled back, but she did not pause. She raced past him, wielded her spear in a dazzling display, surprising Reece as she swung the ten-foot spear around again and again, using it as a staff, knocking out four more of Tirus's men as they tried to take the ship.

He came up beside her, looking out at the damage, all the floating bodies in the water, and both of them stood there, breathing hard, side by side.

"Where did you learn to wield a spear like that?" he asked, impressed.

She shrugged.

"Women on the Upper Isles are not allowed to use swords. So I learned to wield staffs. You don't always need a blade to kill a man."

Several more arrows sailed above their heads, and Reece looked out and saw how close they were to shore now. Waves crashed all around them, and their ship lifted high and was brought low, as the current brought them in at full speed now, riding the waves. They were now hardly twenty yards to shore, and hundreds of Tirus's men, wielding swords, firing arrows, rushed forward to greet them, wading out into the waters. His men, firing back, were falling left and right. It was like walking into a wall of fire.

Reece knew that something needed to be done fast—if they continued like this, they would all be dead before they reached shore.

Reece had an idea; it was bold, and risky, but it was crazy enough that it just might work. He turned to the captain.

"Can you set it aflame?" Reece shouted out.

The captain, just feet away, turned and looked at Reece as if he were crazy. He clearly did not understand.

"Our ship!" Reece called out. "The sails! Light them! Set the whole thing on fire!"

"Are you mad?" the captain shouted back. "So we shall all go up in flames and die?"

Reece shook his head, coming in close, grabbing the captain's arm with urgency as arrows sailed by their heads.

"We shall arrange casks of oil around the center flame. As we get closer, we will let his men board the ship. As they do, we'll jump off the back, and when we're safe in the waters, we'll fire our flaming arrows and burn our ship with Tirus's men aboard!"

Srog, standing nearby, looked at the captain, who looked questioningly back at Srog, both of them uncertain if Reece was mad or a brilliant commander. Finally, arrows whizzing by, they both seemed to decide there was little left to lose, seeing that a certain death lay ahead of them

The captain nodded and began barking orders. His men rushed to follow his command, placing several casks of oil around the mast, and draping the lower sails over them.

Reece led the others in grabbing arrows, wrapping their tips in rags, and soaked them in oil, prepared for flames. They all, as he led them, abandoned their positions and ran to the rear of the ship, giving up the bow to give Tirus's men an opening to board.

They huddled there in the back, waiting, as the current lead them closer and closer to shore. Reece watched as Tirus's men began to board; like ants, they began to crawl over the rails of the bow and drop down to the deck, one after the other.

All his men, crouching, waiting, were fidgety, anxious to jump off the ship.

"Not yet!" Reece commanded.

More and more of Tirus's men stumbled onto the ship, filling the deck, hundreds of men. They began to run across the ship as they spotted them, an army racing to kill them.

"Not yet!" Reece ordered. He wanted the ship to fill with as many of them as possible.

They came closer and closer, nearly reaching them, drawing swords, letting out battle cries, assuming that Reece's men were afraid.

Finally, as the closest soldier was but yards away, Reece screamed, "Fire!"

As one, the Queen's men fired, unleashing dozens of arrows, aflame, for the sails and the casks of oil beneath them. They did not even wait for the arrows to hit; they followed Reece's lead and immediately turned and leapt off the rear of the ship, into the ocean.

As Reece went flying over the edge, he grabbed Stara, and the two of them landed in the water together. The water was freezing, especially as Reece was immersed over his head, but he held onto Stara's hand, and she to his, and while he was underwater, he heard a tremendous explosion which nearly rocked his ears.

Reece's feet hit bottom—luckily only about ten feet deep here— and he bounced back up and surfaced to a spectacle the likes of which he was sure he would never see again. The ship he had just abandoned was exploding, in explosion after explosion, completely aflame, as one cask after another lit up. It lit the mast and the sails and the entire deck and rail, and the whole thing went up so fast, there was no time for Tirus's men to react.

There came the cries of hundreds of men aflame. They leapt from the ship, on fire, but it was too late for most of them.

Reece looked out at the scene with a great sense of satisfaction. He had taken out hundreds of Tirus's men, and had saved all of his men on the ship. They had gone from sure death, to now having a fighting chance.

Reece, bobbing in the waves, turned and looked to the shoreline. Grabbing Stara's hand, he, along with all the others, swam until he was up to his chest; then they began to wade, up to their stomachs, then their knees, as they made their way in the strong tides, waves breaking all around them, for shore.

Yet still, they had no safe haven. Hundreds more of Tirus's soldiers, reinforcements, appeared on shore, and these men, swords raised, charged for them, wading out into the water to greet them.

Reece, his shoulder throbbing, dripping wet, freezing, knee-deep in water, raised his sword with his good arm and rushed out to meet his first foe. He blocked his blow with a grunt, the man twice his size, leaning in for him, then he sidestepped him; the man rushed forward into the water, and Reece spun and slashed him.

All around him, his men fought hand-to-hand, soldier to soldier, trying to fight for each step, to fight their way to shore. They fought fearlessly, fighting for their lives, as the air filled with the clang of metal and the cries of men. Men fell on both sides, and soon the waters ran red with blood.

Still more of Tirus's soldiers arrived on shore, a never-ending stream. With each step Reece gained, with each man he killed, yet another man arrived.

There came a chorus of horns, and Reece turned to see Falus's flotilla bearing down on them, dozens and dozens of huge warships, closing in fast. They were trapped, sandwiched between two foes.

Reece knew he would die on this day; yet at least he took comfort in the fact that he would die on his feet, as a soldier, sword in hand, and would not stop fighting until he could not lift his arms. He might die—but he would bring down all the men that he could with him.

# CHAPTER TWENTY-SIX

As dawn broke, Gwendolyn stood on the bow of her ship, clutching Guwayne, looking out with dread over the gloomy ocean of the Upper Isles. Finally, land had come into view—and yet, that was not what was catching her eye.

Instead of feeling relieved at seeing land, relieved at having made it, Gwen's eyes settled on a much more disturbing view: she saw dozens of warships, bearing Tirus's banners, their backs to them, all sailing for the bay, as if to attack their own island.

At first, Gwen was confused. It made no sense. Why would they be launching an attack on their own people?

Kendrick, Godfrey, Steffen, and all her advisors came up beside her in the early morning sun, all looking out at the same alarming view. And as they sailed closer, as Gwen squinted at the horizon, it all began to make sense. There, trapped in the bay, were about a dozen of her fleet, many of them on fire, plumes of black smoke rising to the horizon. The shouts of dying men could be heard even from here. They were trapped between Tirus's fleet at sea, and his men on shore.

Gwen realized what had happened: Tirus's men were waging an all-out war on the remainder of her fleet. And her men, the few who remained, were getting slaughtered.

As Gwen looked out, she felt certain that her brother Reece was on one of the ships—along with Srog and all of her men. Gwen immediately felt guilty. Clearly, they had held their positions here to honor her command. She felt as if somehow she had let them down, had exposed them to die at the hands of these Upper Islanders.

Gwendolyn felt a wave of panic, and she knew she could not allow this to happen—she could not allow her men to go down in defeat. Whatever the cause, even if Reece had defied her command, even if he should not have murdered Tirus, he was still her brother, and these were still her men. The Upper Islanders could not be allowed to harm them. They needed to learn what happened when you defied the Queen, the Silver, the MacGils; they needed to feel the wrath of the Ring.

Yet Gwendolyn sailed in a vulnerable position, vastly outnumbered by the dozens of large, well-armed ships of the Upper Isles. While Gwendolyn's fighting force was superior, there was clearly no way they could defeat them at sea in a head-on match.

"Not exactly the welcome you expected, is it, sister?" Kendrick asked, looking out with a warrior's visage, remaining calm as he studied the scene with a professional warrior's eye.

"I told you that Tirus was not to be trusted," Godfrey added.

Gwen shook her head.

"None of that matters now," she said. "We create our own welcomes in this world."

Her voice was cold, hardened, the voice of her father—and all her men looked to her with a clear respect.

"But surely, my lady," Aberthol said, "we cannot just attack this vast fleet."

"We bear the element of surprise," Gwendolyn said. "They are not expecting an attack from the rear, from the open sea. They won't be looking for us. By the time they react, we could already have taken out a good portion of their fleet."

"And then what?" Aberthol pressed. "Once they catch on, once they turn and face us, they will crush us at sea."

Gwendolyn realized he was right. She needed a plan, a crafty plan, something to be executed in haste. She could not risk a head-on confrontation.

She scanned the horizon, studied the topography, the jetties jutting out into the sea, the U-shaped basin in which her brother was trapped; she drew on all of her reading of history, of military strategy and tactics, of all her scholarship of a thousand famous battles—and suddenly, she had an idea.

Her eyes lit up with excitement as she realized it was crazy enough that it just might work. What was it her father had told her? *For a commander to win, his plan must be two-thirds logic and one-third madness.*

165

"They're trapping our men in a narrow bay, in a U-shaped passage, between those jetties," Gwendolyn said. "Yet that can work to their disadvantage too. When you trap others, you are also trapped yourself."

They all looked at her, confused.

Godfrey furrowed his brow.

"I do not understand, my lady."

Gwen pointed to the jetties.

"We can trap them," she added

Her men blinked, still not comprehending.

"The ropes," she said hastily, turning to Kendrick. "The spiked ropes. The ones in the hold. How long are they?"

"The ones used for harbor warfare?" Kendrick asked. "At least a hundred yards, my lady."

She nodded as she recalled the ropes she had once seen her father use, endlessly long, with spikes tied to them every few feet, sharp as a sword. She had once seen her father spread the ropes in a harbor, and had watched as the enemy ships sailed over them, and crumbled into pieces.

"Exactly," she said. "Those."

Kendrick shook his head.

"It is a good idea for a condensed fleet," Kendrick said. "But it would never work here. This is open water, not shallow water. Remember, we'll attack them from the sea. The water won't be shallow enough to damage the holds of the ships. Those ropes are placed on a shallow ocean floor."

Gwen shook her head, the idea crystallizing in her mind.

"You don't understand," she said. "Those ropes can be used other ways, too. We needn't drop the ropes on the ocean floor—we can sail close and make the ropes taut in the water, and as they pursue, it will destroy them."

Kendrick stared back, puzzled.

"But how, my lady? How will you get the ropes taut?"

"We shall attack from their rear and set their fleet on fire," she explained. "As they turn to confront this, we will already have the ropes in place. We will launch small boats first, one on either end of the harbor, one led by you, the other by Godfrey. Each will carry one end of the rope, and will tie them to the rocks, to one end of each jetty. You will make them taut, and keep them just below the surface of the water. Tirus's men will be looking at us when they attack—not below the surface for any trap in the water. They will sail into our spikes!"

Kendrick peered out at the horizon, studying the topography, hands on his hips. Slowly, he nodded.

"Is a bold idea," he concluded.

"It is madness!" Aberthol said. "I can think of a hundred things that can go wrong!."

Gwendolyn stepped up and smiled, a fearless commander in her prime:

"And that is exactly why we're going to do it," she said.

*

Gwen stood at the bow, her heart pounding, looking out as her half dozen ships sailed beside her, all of them, at her command, keeping as quiet as could be. Not a sound could be heard save for the howling of the wind and the distant shouts of her men, of Reece and the others, trapped in the bay, fighting for their lives.

Gwendolyn watched with satisfaction as the two small boats, each holding a dozen men, one led by Kendrick, the other by Godfrey, rowed quickly, each holding one end of the rope. Inside their boats were the boldest warriors who had volunteered on the risky mission, among them several Legion—Elden, O'Connor, and Conven, along with several of the new recruits. Steffen wanted to volunteer, but Gwendolyn selfishly kept him here, by her side.

Her fleet approached at full sail, the wind picking up, gaining momentum as they sailed closer and closer to the rear of Tirus's fleet. Gwen held her breath, hoping no one in Tirus's fleet turned around and spotted them.

167

Gwen waited impatiently, clutching Guwayne, as she watched her boats getting into position. They rowed as hard and as quietly as they could, their oars slapping the water, until finally, Kendrick and Godfrey's boats each took their position at the end of each jetty, but yards away from the enemy ships. Immediately, they set about tying each end of the rope to the huge boulders at the end of each jetty. As they did, the rope became taut, briefly rising above the surface, until they slackened it to allow it to be hidden below.

"Bows, prepare!" Gwen commanded to her men onboard.

A host of her men raised their bows, flaming arrows at the ready, awaiting her command.

"Aim for the top sails!" she called out. "As high as you can!"

They sailed closer, and closer, the tension so thick she could cut it with a knife. She had just one shot at this, and she wanted it to be perfect.

They were barely fifty yards away from the rear of Tirus's fleet when, finally, she was ready.

"FIRE!" she cried.

A thousand arrows suddenly filled the air from Gwen's fleet of ships, all aflame, all sailing in a high arc. Gwen held her breath as she watched them lighting up the dawn.

A moment later they landed, blanketing Tirus's fleet.

"FIRE!" she yelled again.

Her men fired volley after volley, flaming arrows lighting up the sky like a plague of locusts, and landing on Tirus's ships.

There arose cries of confusion, and of pain, as some of Tirus's ships suddenly went ablaze. A half dozen ships, in the rear of his fleet, were so badly hit that they went up in a quick succession of flames, men trying frantically to put out the flames, but unsuccessful. They leapt, on fire, into the ocean.

The rest of the fleet, though—dozens more ships—were out of reach of the arrows, or managed to put out the blazes fast enough so that no real damage was done. They all slowly turned around to face Gwendolyn, an army vastly larger than hers. They gave up the chase in the harbor, but now they set their sights on Gwen.

They were intimidating, this well-coordinated fleet of warships bearing down on them, and Gwen knew that if her ropes didn't work, she and her men would be dead within minutes.

Gwendolyn raised her hand and lowered it sharply, the sign she had prepared. As she did, she watched Kendrick and his men yank the heavy rope on one end, and Godfrey and his men on the other. The rope rose higher, just above the water's surface, one hundred yards wide, and they quickly wrapped it around new boulders, again and again, securing it.

They had waited until the last moment, until Tirus's fleet was too close to see the spikes protruding from the water. Tirus's men finally noticed it—but too late.

Tirus's fleet, unsuspecting, sailed right into the trap. The sound of splintering wood tore through the air, followed by the sound of wood groaning. Kendrick and Godfrey and all the Legion boys manned their positions fearlessly, holding onto the ropes with their bare hands, to make sure they didn't loosen. They held on for dear life, groaning against the weight of the ships.

Tirus's fleet continued to lodge itself into the spikes, one after the other, too late to turn around, all lined up side by side in the narrow harbor, all sailing in haste to destroy Gwendolyn. Within moments, the ships began to buckle, then to list. The bows began to nosedive, straight down into the water, as the ships fell apart into a million pieces.

Tirus's men cried out in terror, falling from the off-balance ships, flailing in the ocean as the great currents sucked them down. Within moments, his fleet, sailing so proud, indomitable just moments before, was completely wiped out.

Gwendolyn's men let out a great cheer of victory as Tirus's fleet plummeted down to the depths of the sea.

"ATTACK!" Gwen screamed.

Gwendolyn's men raised the mainsail, and they picked up wind and sailed and rowed with all they had, full speed right into the harbor, to reinforce Reece and what was left of her fleet. As they neared, she could already see Reece and the others wading in the waves up to their knees, fighting hand to hand, outnumbered by all Tirus's men on shore.

That was about to change. A chorus of horns sounded, marking the arrival of Gwen's feet, and Tirus's soldiers on shore began to stop their fighting and look up at the arriving fleet in fear.

"AIM HIGH AND FIRE!" Gwen shouted.

Her men unleashed hundreds more arrows in a high arc, sailing through the air, over the heads of Reece and her men, and striking Tirus's soldiers on shore. Screams filled the air, as one after another soldier dropped to the sand, bloody, as the sky darkened with arrows. Volley after volley rose up and landed, and soon, nearly every man on the beach, save her own, was dead. Whoever remained turned and fled.

Gwen was close enough to see Reece's face as he and the others turned and looked up at her in shock, in awe, and in gratitude.

They had survived. Victory was theirs.

# CHAPTER TWENTY-SEVEN

Romulus stood at the base of the Canyon crossing, his million-man army behind them, and looked out in a seething rage. Up above, his dragons shrieked as they threw themselves, again and again, into Argon's invisible shield blocking the Canyon, infuriated, unable to cross. Romulus looked up, watching, wondering what could have happened, wondering what force could be strong enough to withstand all these dragons.

Romulus knew that he had destroyed the Shield for good—and he had been told by every sorcerer that the Shield would not rise again; that the Ring was his forever; and that no force on earth could stop him.

Romulus did indeed occupy the Ring—his men now occupied every corner of it, on both sides of the Highlands. They had razed every town, reduced them to rubble, to ashes, and there was not a single thing left to rebuild. The Ring belonged to him now. It was now Empire territory.

And yet here Romulus was, unable to leave the Ring, trapped inside, with this invisible Shield that had somehow been erected by Argon. As Romulus peered out across the Bridge, he wondered what had happened here, and how to destroy it. And most of all: where had Gwendolyn escaped to?

Romulus turned to Luanda, who stood by his side.

"Where has your sister gone?" he demanded.

Luanda stood there, no longer bound, finally loyal, not running anywhere. Romulus took satisfaction in seeing her, a woman he thought he would never break, once so fiercely independent, now subservient to his will, like everybody else. All of his beatings had worked; she was now like every other slave, ready to do his bidding. One day, he might even marry her—and when he'd had enough of her, he'd kill her just as quickly. Of course, she did not know that yet. She would be in for a rude surprise.

Luanda looked out at the horizon, and seemed to be thinking.

"She wouldn't try to make a home in the Wilds," she replied. "She would know there is no home for her there. She must be bringing her people to the ships; she must have had them prepared. There is only one place she could sail that is close, friendly territory, a place she probably would not think you would ever venture. A place hidden in the stormy northern seas: the Upper Isles."

Romulus examined the Canyon crossing, saw the footprints of thousands across it, and he wondered. If he could get past this shield, he would take half of his million man army, lead them to his ships, and set off for the Upper Isles. He would surround every inch of it, and destroy it to oblivion.

First, though, he would send his host of dragons across the ocean, would command them to set it all to fire before his arrival. He would arrive on an island flattened by devastation. He would not even need to raise a sword.

The dragons shrieked again and again, and Romulus knew he had to bring down this new Shield, to undo Argon's handiwork. Romulus threw his head back, threw his arms out wide, opened his palms, faced the sky, and shrieked, summoning all of his newfound energy, more determined than ever. If he could summon dragons, he could summon the darkest energies of hell to do his bidding.

There came a great thunder, the earth quaked, and shafts of black light shot down from the heavens, into Romulus's palms. They glowed and vibrated, as he felt the energy passing through him, and down into the earth.

"Ancient powers, I summon you!" Romulus shrieked. "Shatter this shield!"

Romulus opened his eyes, directed his palms forward, and with a great shriek directed all the black light to the invisible shield before him.

Argon's shield was suddenly covered in black light, spreading over it, more and more vibrant, until finally the shield began to crack.

Suddenly, there came a huge explosion.

The invisible shield exploded into a million little pieces, sprinkling down like snow all around them. Romulus looked up, amazed, feeling the minuscule fragments rain all around him, in his hair, and settling, like dust, in his open palms.

The dragons screeched in victory as they no longer butted against an invisible wall, but flew forward, racing through the open air, across the Canyon, out toward the Wilds.

Romulus leaned back and laughed in delight, knowing that soon the dragons would cross the Wilds, would cross the ocean, would descend upon Gwendolyn and her men and destroy every last one of them.

He would follow on their heels.

"Fly, my dragons," he laughed. "Fly."

# CHAPTER TWENTY-EIGHT

Erec stood on a plateau in the cliffs, overlooking the contest going on before him, cheers rising up as hundreds of men sparred before him. Perhaps twenty feet below was a wide plateau, fifty yards in diameter, shaped in a perfect circle, a steep drop off all around it. A massive copper gate was erected around its perimeter, rising a good ten feet high, assuring that no warriors would fall over the edge and that none of these matches would result in death.

Yet it was still a serious business. This day's contests dictated who had the right to challenge Erec for the kingship in the wake of his father's death. All of these fine warriors, brothers in arms, all of the same nation and the same island, were not here to kill each other. The weapons were blunted today, and the armor was extra plated. But they all wanted to be King, and they all wanted to prove their skills on the field of battle.

As Erec watched over them, admiring their skills, his mind swarmed with a million thoughts. He was still processing his father's last words, all he had told him about ruling a nation. Erec wondered if he was really up to the task. He looked down at all these fine warriors, at the thousands of people lining the cliffs, watching, all of them so noble, and he wondered why he should be the one to rule them.

Most of all, Erec marveled at the fact that his father had just died, and yet here were all these people, celebrating, going on as if nothing had happened. Erec himself swarmed with conflicting emotions. A part of him could understand his people's traditions, to celebrate the life of his father, instead of mourn him; after all, mourning could not bring him back. Yet another part of him wanted time and space to mourn the man he barely knew.

"Many will fight you, my brother," Strom said, grinning, coming up beside him and patting Erec heartily on the back. "And I will be first among them."

174

Erec turned and saw the royal family beside him—Strom, Dauphine, his mother, Alistair at his side—all of them up here on this vantage point, looking down on the contests. Below there came the clang of metal, as hundreds of great warriors faced off with each other, one at a time, eliminating each other. They had been fighting like this for hours, determined to dwindle their ranks down to the twelve victors who would be left to fight Erec for the kingship.

As was the tradition, the dozen victors would represent the dozen provinces of the Islands, and each of them would have a chance to fight Erec. It would allow each province to be represented, as each province fought it out for their own individual victor. It gave each and every person on the island a chance to challenge for the kingship, the same way his ancestors had done for centuries. These twelve victors would represent the best that the people had to offer, and while, of course, Erec would be tired fighting twelve men, it was still the test of a true warrior. If he could defeat them all, back to back, then his people would be satisfied to recognize him as King.

Strom laughed again.

"You have long been away from these islands," he added, "and I have been training for this for years. Don't be too sad when I beat you!"

Strom patted Erec on the back and laughed heartily, delighted with himself. Erec looked his brother up and down and saw that he would indeed be a formidable foe. He had no doubt he was a fine warrior, with the finest armor, and trained by the finest of his father's people. And he had no doubt that his brother dearly wanted the kingship—and most of all, dearly wanted to defeat him.

"Do not worry, my brother," Erec replied. "You shall have a chance to fight me, along with everyone else."

Strom smiled.

"Do not be disappointed if you find yourself calling me King before the day's close."

Strom laughed, and Erec smiled to himself. His brother was bold and confident, he always had been. But of course, that could also lead to a warrior's undoing.

175

Erec turned his attention back to the fighting, studying them with a warrior's eye. The matches went on and on, the air filled with the cries and groans of men, and with the sound of clanging metal. Warriors charged each other on horses at a full gallop and raised their lances high, jousting. The custom of the Southern Islanders, Erec knew, was that one must win both on horse and on foot—so after the men went down, the battles always morphed to hand-to-hand combat. The warriors here, after all, were tested more thoroughly than any warriors in the world.

As hours passed and the sun fell long in the sky, the last of the provinces declared a victor; finally, a chorus of horns sounded, and the people let out a great cheer.

The twelve victors of the day were lined up, fierce warriors each, all ready to fight Erec for the right to be King.

"Looks like it's our turn, my brother!" Strom said, donning his helmet and hurrying down the stone steps.

Erec grabbed his armor, kissed Alistair, and followed him down. As Erec approached the arena, the sky grew thick with the shouts of thousands of islanders, all thrilled to welcome him, and to watch him fight the others.

Erec noticed Strom getting ready to spar, and he was confused.

"But I shall fight you last," Erec said, catching up to him. "That is tradition."

Strom shook his head.

"Not anymore," he replied. "I've changed the rules. You will fight me first. I must defeat you right away, so that I can then defeat all the others. After all, once I'm King, I will have proved to all these people that I'm a better fighter than you. That is, unless you are afraid to fight me first."

Erec shook his head at his younger brother's confidence.

"I back down from no challenge," Erec replied.

"Do not worry," Strom said, "I'll try not to hurt you in the process!"

176

Strom laughed at his own joke, thrilled with himself, and ran and mounted his horse, grabbing his lance and heading into the sparring ring.

Erec mounted the beautiful horse laid out for him, looked down, and examined three lances being held out. He weighed each one, and finally settled on one, shorter than the others, and lighter, with a copper hilt. He had barely grabbed hold of it when already his brother was charging for him.

Erec charged, too, and now that he was in fighting mode, something snapped inside of him. He transformed into a professional soldier, and he no longer saw the man riding toward him as his brother. Now he was his opponent.

Everything else fell away as he focused with laser-like clarity. As had happened his entire life, something changed inside him once he lowered his faceplate and charged, something he could not control. He became a machine, intent on defeating anyone who stood in his way, brother or not.

Erec let go of all emotions, of all feelings of competition or jealousy or envy. He knew these would only get in his way. For the professional warrior, there was no room to allow one's mind to be clouded by emotion.

Instead, as he lowered his lance, as he heard the sound of his own breathing in his ears, Erec focused on every tiny motion of his brother—the shifting armor, where he held his lance. His brother was confident, he could see it in the way he rode. He could also see that that was his weakness.

As they neared, at the last moment, Erec made a tiny adjustment; he raised his lance a bit higher, shifted his body to the right, and struck his lance into his brother's chest.

There came a great clang as his brother went flying off the back of his horse and landed on his back. The crowd cheered.

Erec circled around, seeing his brother lying on the ground, groaning, rolling to get up. He dismounted and stood there, waiting, giving his brother time. He felt bad; this was his brother after all.

Strom quickly rose to his feet, pulled off his helmet, his face red with fury, and screamed to his squire: "MACE!"

Erec stood opposite him, calm and cool, as he removed his helmet and took the mace handed to him from his own squire. These were large wooden maces, their studs blunted so as not to kill—but still, their impact would be felt.

"A lucky strike!" Strom yelled. "You shall not do it twice!"

Strom charged and screamed, swinging wildly. They were powerful blows—but blows clouded by emotion. Erec, focused, was able to deftly deflect each one.

Strom paused, breathing hard, and glared back.

"I'll give you one chance to yield to me now!" Strom called out. "Yield now, and proclaim me King!"

Erec shook his head at his brother's confidence. Although his brother was deadly serious, Erec could not help smiling.

"You are gracious to offer me the chance," Ere called back. "But it is too kind. It is a chance I cannot accept. I did not choose to be King; I do not desire to be King; but I shall never yield in combat— not to any man, and not even to my brother."

Strom shouted and charged like a madman, raising his mace to strike a great blow upon Erec's head.

Erec turned his mace sideways, raised it high, and blocked the blow. He then leaned forward and kicked his brother in the chest, sending him flying back, landing on his rear on the ground.

Erec then charged forward, swung his mace around, and as Strom raised his mace to block it, Erec swung from underneath and managed to strike the head of Strom's mace perfectly, and sent the mace flying from his brother's hand. It went flying over the copper railing, over the edge of the arena, and down the side of the cliff.

Erec stood over his defenseless brother, the mace pointed at his throat.

Strom looked back, wide-eyed, clearly not expecting this at all.

"I love you, my brother," Erec said. "I do not wish to harm you. End this now, and our match is over with no bruises or scratches."

But Strom glared back at him.

178

"Another lucky blow," Strom seethed. "Do you really think I would bow to my lesser in battle?"

Strom suddenly scrambled to his knees and charged for him, aiming to tackle Erec by his legs.

Erec saw it coming and sidestepped, letting his brother go barreling forward. As he did, Erec reached up and with his foot shoved him, sending him flying face-first in the dirt.

Strom rolled to his feet, face filled with hate as the crowd laughed at him.

"Sword!" Strom called out to his squire. "A REAL sword!"

The crowd gasped, as his squire rushed forward with the sword, then stopped and looked to Erec for approval.

Erec glared back at Strom, hardly believing what he was seeing, disappointed in him.

"My brother, this is a friendly contest," he said, calmly. "Sharpened weapons should not be used."

"I demand a real sword!" he called out, frantic. "Unless you are afraid to meet me in battle!"

Erec sighed, seeing there was no stopping his brother. He would just have to learn.

Erec nodded to the attendant, who handed Strom a sword, as Erec stood there, facing him.

"And where is your sword?" Strom asked, as he gained his feet.

Erec shook his head.

"I do not need one. In fact, I do not even need this."

Erec dropped his mace, and the crowd gasped. He stood there defenseless, facing his brother.

"Should I kill a defenseless man?" his brother said.

"A true knight is never defenseless. Only one clouded with emotion is defenseless."

Strom looked back, confused; he was clearly struggling, wondering whether he should attack a defenseless man. But finally his ambition got the best of him; his face collapsed in rage, and with a shout, he raised his sword and charged Erec.

Erec waited, biding his time, gauging his brother's strength, then dodged out of the way at the last moment; the blade swished by his ear, just missing. Erec was disappointed, realizing that his brother truly had intent to kill.

In the same motion, without missing a beat, Erec reached around and elbowed his brother in the small of his back, where he had no armor. Strom cried out as Erec hit the pressure point he was hoping for, right beneath his kidney, and he dropped to his knees, dropping the sword.

Erec spun, kicked him in the back, sending him to his face, and stood on the back of his neck, keeping his face planted in the dirt. He stood more firmly than before, letting his brother know he'd had enough.

"You have lost, brother," Erec said. "This spur is sharper than the blade of your sword. If you move but half an inch, it will sever every artery in your throat. Do you really want our fight to continue?"

The crowd fell silent, everyone riveted as they watched the two brothers.

Finally, Strom, breathing hard, shook his head slightly.

"Then declare it," Erec said. "Yield!"

Strom lay there for several moments in the silence, not one person making a move, until finally he screamed out: "I YIELD!"

There came a great roar, and Erec lifted his foot from his brother's throat. Strom, unharmed, got to his feet and stormed away, his back to Erec, not even turning back once, his face covered in mud.

A horn sounded, followed by a great cheer.

"And now, the twelve victors!"

Erec turned and saw the victors from the dozen provinces, lined up in respect, all waiting their turn to fight him.

He knew this would be a long afternoon indeed.

\*

Erec jousted for hours, with one knight after another, his shoulders growing tired, his eyes stinging with sweat. By the afternoon's end, even his sword was feeling heavy to the touch.

Erec fought one victor at a time, each from another province, each a fierce warrior. And yet, none were a match for him. One after the next, he'd defeat each one at the joust, and then each in hand-to-hand combat.

But the more fights he had, the fiercer and more accomplished the warriors became—and the more tired he became. This was truly a test of kings: to win, one had to be not only the best fighter, but also have the most stamina to fight off all twelve of the best men these islands had to offer. It was one thing to beat a challenger for the first fight of the day; it was quite another to beat him on the twelfth fight.

And yet, Erec persevered. He summoned all his years of training, of battle, of long bouts of fighting one man after the next, recalling those days when the Silver were challenged beyond extremes, having to fight not just a dozen men, but two dozen, three dozen—even a hundred men in a single day. They would fight until their arms were too tired to even raise a sword, and still have to find some way to win. That was the training King MacGil had demanded.

Now, it served him well. Erec summoned his skill, his instincts, and even in exhaustion, he fought better than all these great warriors, the greatest warriors in a kingdom known for the greatest warriors. Erec outshone them all, and with a dazzling display of virtuosity, he defeated one after the next. A horn punctuated each victory, and a satisfied cheer from his people, clearly feeling assured that they had, in their new King to be, the greatest warrior their islands had to offer.

As Erec defeated the eleventh challenger with a blow of his wooden mace on the man's ribs, the man yielded, the eleventh horn sounded, and the crowd went wild.

Erec stood there, breathing hard, reaching down to give the warrior a hand up.

"Well fought," the warrior said, a man twice his size.

"You fought bravely," Erec said. "I shall make you commander of one of my legions."

The man clasped Erec's arm in respect, and turned and walked off to his people, proud and noble in defeat.

The crowd cheered wildly, as Erec turned toward the twelfth and final victor. The man mounted his horse on the far side of the arena and faced him. The crowd would not stop cheering, knowing that after this battle, they would have their King.

Erec mounted his horse, breathing hard, drinking from a cup of water brought to him by one of his squires, then dumping the rest of the cold water on his head. Erec then raised his helmet and put it back on his head, wiping the sweat from his brow as he grabbed a fresh lance.

Erec surveyed the knight facing him. He was twice as wide as the others, and wore copper armor with three streaks of black across it. Erec's stomach clenched at the sight; those marks were worn by a small tribe, the Alzacs, in the southernmost part of the island, a separatist tribe that had been a thorn in his father's side for years. They were the fiercest warriors of the island, and one of them had been King before his father. It was an Alzac that his father had had to defeat in order to seize the throne so many years ago.

"I am Bowyer of the Alzacs!" the knight called out to Erec. "Your father took the throne from my father forty sun cycles ago. Now I shall avenge my father and take the throne from you. Prepare to kneel to your new King!"

Bowyer's head was stark bald, and he had a short, stiff brown beard. He sat erect on his horse, with a defiant face and the flattened nose of a warrior who had seen battle.

Erec knew the Alzacs to be fierce and brave—and sneaky. He was not surprised that this was the final fighter left, the champion of the victors. Erec knew it would not be easy and that this challenger should not be underestimated. He would take nothing for granted.

Erec focused as a horn sounded, visors were lowered, and the two galloped for each other.

They charged and as their lances met, Erec was surprised to feel Bowyer's lance impact his chest, the first of the day; at the same time, Erec's lance impacted his. Bowyer had made an unexpected last-second twist, and Erec realized that Bowyer was indeed finer than any he had yet encountered. The blow was not hard enough to knock Erec off his horse, but he did sway backwards, his confidence shaken.

Bowyer, too, remained on his horse, and they circled around to face each other again, to the cheers of the crowd. Bowyer, too, seemed surprised that Erec had impacted him, and they both charged each other with a new respect.

This time, as they neared, Erec had a better feel for Bowyer's rhythms. That, indeed, was one of Erec's strengths: being able to sum up his enemy and adjust quickly. This time, Erec waited until the last moment, then lowered his lance just a bit, a move Bowyer could not have expected, as he aimed for Bowyer's rib cage.

It was a perfect strike, and Erec managed to knock Bowyer sideways off his horse; he hit the ground hard, tumbling in a clang of armor.

The crowd cheered wildly as Erec circled around, dismounted, and removed his helmet.

Bowyer rolled to his feet, his face purple with rage, a look of death in his eyes unlike any he had seen today. Others had clearly wanted to win; but Bowyer, Erec could see, wanted to kill.

"If you are a real man," Bowyer boomed out, loud enough for all to hear, "and you are aspiring to be a *real* King, let us fight with real weapons! I demand to use real swords in combat! And I demand the gates to be lowered."

The crowd gasped at Bowyer's words.

Erec looked at the copper gates around the perimeter of the sparring field, the only thing separating them from the cliffs below. He knew what lowering them meant: it meant a fight to the death.

"Do you request a match to the death?" Erec asked.

"I do!" Bowyer boomed. "I demand it!"

The crowd gasped. Erec stood there, debating; he did not want to kill this man, but he could not back down.

Bowyer boomed out: "Unless you are afraid!"

Erec blushed.

"I fear no man," he called out, "and I refuse no challenge in combat. If it is your wish, then lower the gates."

The crowd gasped, and a horn sounded, and slowly, several attendants turned massive cranks. A groaning noise filled the air, and inch by inch, the copper gates that surrounded the arena lowered. A wind rushed through, and now there was nothing left to stop the warriors from going over the edge, from plummeting to their deaths. Now, there was no room for error. Erec had seen matches as a youth with the gates lowered—and they had always ended in death.

Bowyer, wasting no time, grabbed a real sword from his squire and charged. Erec grabbed his. As he neared Erec, Bowyer swung his sword with both hands for Erec's head, a death blow; Erec raised his sword to block it, sparks flying.

Erec spun with his own blow, and Bowyer blocked it. Then Bowyer slashed back.

Back and forth they went, slashing and parrying, attacking, blocking, defending, sparks flying, swords whistling through the air, clanging, as they went blow for blow for blow. Erec was exhausted from the day's battle, and Bowyer was a formidable opponent, fighting as if his life depended on it.

The two did not stop as they drove each other back and forth, back and forth, getting close to the edge, then farther from it, ebbing and flowing, each circling the other, trying to drive him back, trying to gain advantage.

Finally, Erec landed a perfectly placed blow, slashing sideways and knocking Bowyer's sword from his hand. Bowyer blinked, confused, then rushed to get it, diving down to the dirt.

Erec stood over him and raised his visor.

"Yield!" Erec said, as Bowyer lay there, prone.

Bowyer, though, grabbed a handful of dirt, spun and, before Erec could see it coming, threw it in Erec's face.

Erec shouted out, blinded, raising his hands to his eyes as they stung, and dropping his sword. Bowyer did not hesitate; he charged, tackling him, driving him all the way across the arena, right to the edge of the cliff, and tackling him down to the ground.

The crowd gasped as Erec lay on his back, Bowyer on top of him, Erec's head over the edge of the precipice. Erec turned and glanced down, and he knew that if he moved just inches, he would plummet to his death.

Erec looked up to see Bowyer grimacing down, death in his eyes. He lowered his thumbs to gouge out Erec's eyes.

Erec reached up and grabbed Bowyer's wrists, and it was like grabbing onto live snakes. They were all muscle, and it took every ounce of Erec's strength just to hold Bowyer's fists away.

Groaning, the two of them locked in a struggle, neither giving an inch, Erec knew he had to do something quickly. He knew that he had crossed the tipping point, and that if he resisted anymore, he would lose what little strength he had left.

Instead, Erec decided to make a bold, counterintuitive move: instead of trying to lean forward and get away from the edge, he slumped backwards, over it.

As Erec stopped resisting, all of Bowyer's weight came rushing forward; Erec pulled Bowyer toward him, straight down, and Bowyer flipped upside down over the edge of the cliff, his feet going over his head as Erec hung onto his wrists. Erec rolled onto his stomach, holding on to Bowyer's hands, and then turned and looked down. Bowyer dangled over the edge of the cliff, nothing between him and death but Erec's grip. The crowd gasped.

Erec had turned the tables, and now Bowyer groaned and flailed.

"Don't let go," Bowyer pleaded. "I shall die if you do."

"And yet it was you who wanted the gates lowered," Erec reminded him. "Why should I not give you the same death you hoped for me?"

Bowyer looked at him, panic in his face, as Erec let go of one hand. Bowyer dropped a few inches, as Erec now held just one hand.

"I yield to you!" Bowyer called up to him. "I yield!" he boomed.

The crowd cheered as Erec lay there, holding him, debating.

Finally, Erec decided to spare Bowyer from death. He reached out, grabbed him by the back of the shirt, and pulled him up onto safe ground.

The crowd cheered again and again, as all twelve horns sounded, and they rushed in, crowding Erec, embracing. He stood there, exhausted, depleted of energy, and yet relieved and happy to be so embraced, so loved, by his people. Alistair rushed forward through the crowd, and he embraced her.

He had won. Finally, he would be King.

# CHAPTER TWENTY-NINE

Gwendolyn stood in Tirus's former fort and looked out over his former courtyard, at the swinging body of Tirus's son, Falus. He hung by a noose from his neck in the city's center, dozens of Upper Islanders, citizens who did not protest the rebellion, standing below, looking up, gawking. Gwen was glad that they were; she wanted to send them all a message.

Falus represented the last of the rebellious offspring of Tirus's family, the last of the people Gwen had executed as she had rounded up all surviving rebels here on the Upper Isles. As she watched his body swing, she realized she should have rounded them all up—especially Tirus—long ago. She had been a young and naïve ruler, she realized, putting too much stock in the hope for peace. For way too long she had given Tirus too many chances to survive. She had tried to avoid conflict at all costs—but in doing so, she realized, she had ultimately only generated more conflict. She should have acted boldly and ruthlessly from the start.

As she watched the body swing amidst the cold fog and dark clouds of the Upper Isles, she mused that just moons ago such a sight would have upset her; now, though, since Thor had left her, since she had a child, since she had survived being Queen, something inside her had hardened, and she watched the body swing without the slightest bit of emotion. That scared her. Was she losing sight of who she was? Who was she becoming?

"My lady?" Kendrick asked, standing beside her.

She turned and faced him, snapping out of it.

"Shall we take down the body?"

Gwen looked over and saw her people all around her in the great hall, all of them, after their bold victory, after her fearless decisions in the face of adversity, after her saving them from the hands of Romulus, now looking to her as a great leader and Queen. There were

187

Kendrick, Aberthol, Steffen, Elden, O'Connor, Conven—all the brave men who had fought with her to gain this place back. And amongst them, it warmed her heart to see, now stood Reece, Stara beside him. He was wounded, but intact, and while in the past the sight of him had made her angry, now she was so grateful he was alive.

Gwen turned back to the window, realizing they were all awaiting her decision. She watched the body swing, the last of them, the only one that had not yet been taken down. Across the courtyard, she watched with satisfaction as the old banner of the Upper Isles was lowered, and the new banner of the MacGils was raised. This was her territory now.

"No," Gwen replied, her voice cold and firm. "Let it hang until the sun falls. Let the Upper Islanders know who rules this island now."

"Yes, my lady," he answered. "And what of the remainder of Tirus's soldiers? We have nearly one hundred of them in captivity."

Since they had taken the Isles, Gwen had her men systematically rounded up all Upper Islander soldiers left alive, anyone that might be loyal to Tirus. She would take no chances this time.

She turned and faced him, and tone turned hard.

"Kill them all," she commanded.

Kendrick looked at the men, who looked back at him, all of them wary.

"My lady, is that humane?" Aberthol asked.

Gwen looked at him, cold and hard.

"Humane?" she repeated. "Was it humane for them to betray us, to slaughter our men?"

Aberthol said nothing.

"I have tried to be humane. Many times. But I have learned there is little room for humanity when one is at war. I wish it were otherwise."

She turned to Kendrick.

"The only ones who shall be left to live will be those who never raised a weapon against us. The citizens. I have no resources to hold prisoners, nor the will to hold them. Nor do I trust them. Kill them at once."

"Yes, my lady," Kendrick replied.

Gwendolyn surveyed all the faces, saw them looking back at her with a new respect, and she felt so proud of them for all they had accomplished, that they were all standing there alive on this day.

"I want you all to know how proud of you I am," she said. "You won this island in a glorious battle. You fought fearlessly, and we have a new home here now, thanks to all of you. You faced death, and you fought right through it."

The men nodded gratefully, and Reece stepped forward and lowered his head.

"My Queen," he said. She could hear in his tone that he was finally speaking to her as a ruler, and not as a sister. "I must apologize for starting all this. I do not apologize for killing Tirus, but I do apologize for the lost lives of our men."

She looked at him, cold and hard.

"Do not defy my command again," she said.

Reece nodded, humbled.

"Yes, my lady."

She could see he was contrite, and her expression softened.

"But I must say, you were not wrong to kill Tirus," she admitted. "He deserved it long ago. In fact, it is I who must apologize for not killing him sooner."

Reece looked up at her, nodding back with a new understanding and respect.

Cheers suddenly rose up from down below, and Gwen looked out the window to see thousands of her people, those whom she had evacuated from the Ring, filling the courtyards, entering the deserted homes and taverns, taking homes for themselves.

"Our people seem happy to be here," Godfrey said.

"They are happy to be alive," Gwen corrected. "Life here is better than no life at all."

"You should be very proud, my sister," Kendrick said. "You saved them."

Gwen nodded, but sighed, her heart heavy as she pondered all that they left behind—and all of the looming dangers.

"This could be a new home for us," Godfrey said.

Gwen shook her head.

"I would like to think so," she said. "But we're only safe here as long as Argon's shield holds. But if Argon's spell should falter, then all you see here is fleeting. Then there will be nothing in the world that can stop the devastation that would come."

"But surely Romulus will be content with what he has," Godfrey said. "After all, he has the Ring now. He has everything he wants."

Gwendolyn shook her head, knowing Romulus too well.

"The Ring was never what he wanted," she said. "What he's wanted, what they've always wanted, is our complete destruction. And he will follow us to the ends of the earth to have it."

"And what are the chances of Argon's shield holding then?" Kendrick asked.

"Only Argon can say," Gwen said.

"You know him best," Reece said. "Will he waken?"

Gwendolyn turned to him.

"There's only one way to find out," she said, determined to go and find out.

*

Reece stood with Stara atop the highest cliffs of the Upper Isles, the two of them having hiked here together in silence. With everything now at peace in the Upper Isles, there was little left to do but settle in, and perhaps wait for the invasion to come. The feeling in the air was peaceful—and somber—and when Stara had asked Reece if he'd wanted to take a walk, he was quick to agree. He needed something to distract him from the events that might come—and deep down, a part of him, he had to admit, wanted to be with her. He hated himself for it, and yet he had to admit it was true. They had been through too much together for it to be otherwise.

Yet neither of them had said a word since. They had hiked for nearly an hour, and it became clear to them both that, while they were comfortable with each other's company, this was not a romantic walk. It was a somber walk, a walk of reflection, of understanding.

Reece looked about and found it ironic that the same island they had hiked but moons ago, once overflowing with summer bounty, was now whipped by a cold, bleak wind, blanketed by a gray sky with dark, rolling clouds. Could life change so quickly? he wondered. Could anyone hang onto anything?

Reece began to feel uncomfortable in their heavy silence; he didn't know what to say to her. She apparently had nothing to say to him either, and he began to wonder why she wanted to take the walk at all. He had gone with her to get away from all the death that had surrounded him, to clear his mind.

As they reached the highest plateau of the cliffs, they finally came to a stop beside a small lake, from which there trickled a gentle stream, winding its way down the mountain.

Reece watched, puzzled, as Stara knelt down, reached into her sack, and pulled out a large black flower shaped like a bowl, with a small candle in its center. He wondered what she was doing.

"Is that a mourning candle?" he asked.

Stara nodded.

"I know that things can never be the same between us," she said softly, her voice somber. "That is not why I invited you here. I invited you up here to tell you that I'm sorry for all that happened to Selese. Most of all, I want to tell Selese that I'm sorry, too. Wherever she is."

Reece looked down in shame, as his eyes welled with tears.

"I never meant for anything bad to become her," Stara said. "You must believe me. I *need* you to believe me."

Reece nodded.

"I do," he said. "And I never meant for anything bad, either," he said, as he wiped a tear from his cheek.

"And yet, I was selfish," she said, "selfish to try to steal you away. My actions were selfish. And they were wrong."

She sighed.

191

"They say if you light a mourning candle here, in this pond, and the current takes it down the stream of tears, it will provide solace to the dead," she said. "That is why I invited you here."

Stara took out two flint rocks and lit the candle with the spark. It glowed in the center of the black flower, eerie and surreal.

She held it out to Reece.

"Do you want to place it?" she asked.

Reece gently took the flower from her, the candle burning inside, and their fingers touched as he did. Then he knelt down and gently placed it into the small pond. The waters were icy to his fingers.

Reece stood beside Stara and watched as it floated in the pond. It went nowhere, as there was no breeze up here in this sheltered spot.

"Selese," Reece said, lowering his head. "I love you. Please forgive me."

"Please forgive us," Stara added.

The flower began to float out, just a little bit further, yet it was still not picked up by the stream.

"I know we can never be together," Stara said to Reece. "Not after all this. But at least we can be together in this—in our mourning for Selese."

Stara held out one hand, and Reece took it. They stood there, side-by-side, staring out at the candle, as they lowered their heads and closed their eyes.

Reece prayed for blessings for Selese. And most of all, for forgiveness.

Reece opened his eyes as suddenly a wind picked up, and he watched in surprise as the flower suddenly moved, shifting across the pond before being picked up by the current.

Reece watched in amazement as the current took it into the Stream of Tears. It wound its way down the mountain, twisting and turning.

Reece turned and watched as the water carried it down the mountain face, until finally it was out of sight.

192

Reece turned to look at Stara, and she turned and looked at him. They continue to hold hands—and for some reason, despite their best efforts, neither seemed able to let go.

*

Gwendolyn walked across quickly across the courtyard of her new court, flanked by several of her men. She proceeded through the ancient, stone gates out of the courtyard, and took winding, rocky paths into the countryside, bracing herself against the wind and the rain. But she would not stop for anything. She was determined to see Argon and, once again, to see if she could rouse him.

The path finally led her up a small hill, and as Gwendolyn looked up, she was reassured at the sight of Ralibar. He had finally returned, depositing Argon's limp body, and had sat guard over it ever since.

Gwendolyn reached the top of the plateau, a cold gust of wind whipping her face, and she looked up at Ralibar. He sat there, wings held out, staring back at her as he sat guard over the body of Argon, who lay at his feet, unmoving.

Gwendolyn looked up into Ralibar's soulful eyes.

"Where have you been, my friend?" she asked. "We could have used you in the open sea."

Ralibar purred, flapped his wings gently, and moved his nose up and down. She could feel him going through one of his moods, an emotional storm. She knew he was distraught by something, but she could not understand what he was communicating.

"Will you stay, my friend?" she asked. "Or will you leave us again?"

He lowered his head and rubbed his nose against her hand as she held it out, blinking slowly and making an odd purring noise. She did not understand him; she never had, and she knew she never would. She never knew when he might disappear, or when he might come to her aid, despite how close the two had become. She had concluded that the ways of dragons were inscrutable to her.

She stroked Ralibar's scales, his long nose—and at first he seemed content. But then he surprised her by suddenly flapping his great wings, shrieking and rising up into the air, his talons barely missing her head as he flapped.

She turned and watched him fly off into the horizon. She wondered where he was going, and if he would ever return. He was a greater mystery to her than ever.

Gwendolyn turned her attention to Argon's limp body. She knelt down beside him and stroked his timeless face. It was frozen, cold to the touch.

"Argon," she said. "Can you hear me?"

He did not move.

Gwendolyn turned, saw her men standing behind her, and raised a hand. She sensed that Argon needed to be alone with her.

"Please," she said. "Leave us."

Her men did as she commanded, and Gwen soon found herself kneeling alone on this plateau, beside Argon, the wind howling. She reached up and pulled back his hood, examining his face.

"Please, Argon," she said. "Come back to me."

Still, nothing.

Gwen felt a tear roll down her cheek; she felt a sense of impending doom, and she felt so helpless, and more alone than ever, here in this foreign place.

"I need you, Argon," she pleaded. "Now, more than ever."

There came a long silence, as a cold gust of wind stung her cheeks—then finally, the rain stopped. As it did, Gwen looked down and her heart soared to see Argon's eyes fluttering.

Then, slowly he opened them.

Gwen's heart leapt as he looked at her. His eyes shone with such intensity, she nearly had to look away. She stared down at him in wonder.

"Argon," she said, laughing with relief, so overjoyed he was alive.

She reached down and clasped his hand with both of hers.

"Are you okay?" she asked.

He nodded gently, and she wondered.

"Where are you, Argon? Are you here with me?"

"Partly," he replied.

She sensed that their time together was short, and that she might lose him again. She felt a burning desire to have her questions answered.

"Argon, your shield," she said, "you must tell me: will it last? Please. Just answer me this. Will it last?"

There was a long silence, so long that Gwen suspected he would never reply.

And then, finally, Argon shook his head softly.

As he did, Gwen's heart dropped.

"No," he declared. "Even now, it is destroyed."

Gwen's heart plummeted as she pondered the ramifications. It meant that everything would be destroyed: this island, her people—everything. Her entire life, everyone she loved.

Her breath caught in her throat, as her hands trembled.

"Is there any way to restore it?" she asked. "Any way to protect this place?"

Argon shook his head weakly.

"My Shield—and the Ring—are destroyed forever."

Gwen's blood ran cold. She hardly knew what to say.

"Even now Romulus's dragons approach," Argon added. "And one million of his men."

Gwen's heart was pounding, and she found her hands running cold.

"How can we stop them?" she asked.

Argon shook his head.

"You can't," he said. "Soon, very soon, this island will be destroyed."

Gwen burst into tears.

"And what of Thorgrin?" she asked, between tears. "Will he return to us? Will he help save us?"

Argon waited a long time, then finally shook his head.

"I'm sorry," he said. "He has his own destiny."

Gwendolyn found herself still crying, wiping back tears, despite her best efforts.

"And what of my baby?" she asked. "What of Guwayne?"

Argon remained silent, expressionless, as he closed his eyes. Gwen's heart pounded, wondering if she'd lost him.

"Argon," Gwen pleaded, clutching his arm, "answer me. Please. I beg you."

Argon opened his eyes again and stared right at her.

"You made a choice," he said. "In the Netherworld. I am sorry. But vows exact a toll."

Gwen sobbed, unable to hold back her tears.

"You're been a marvelous Queen," he said. "Your people have lived far longer than they were destined. But even for the best of Queens, the time comes. You cannot always outrun destiny."

Finally, Gwen, devastated, composed herself.

"Is there nothing left to do then but prepare to die?" she asked, desperate.

Argon was silent a long time, until finally, he nodded.

"I'm sorry," he said. "But sometimes, that is all we have."

## CHAPTER THIRTY

Luanda stood on Romulus's ship, not far from him, watching his back as he watched the sea, hands on hips, smiling, victorious. Luanda heard the incessant screeching, and she looked up and watched the host of dragons on the horizon, leading the way, disappearing as they headed north toward the Upper Isles, on their way to destroy her sister and all her people.

Romulus laughed and laughed as he led the fleet of ships, thousands of them, blanketing the sea like a school of fish, sailing away from the Ring for the Upper Isles. Luanda looked out at the horizon, and knew that she should feel satisfaction. After all, she had finally gotten what she'd wanted. The Ring was destroyed; she was avenged. Avenged for Bronson, avenged for her exile from King's Court. Avenged for never being treated the way she deserved to be; avenged for being skipped over for the youngest. She had avenged herself on everyone who had doubted her, on everyone who had cast her off as meaningless.

But Luanda was surprised to realize that she did not feel triumphant; she did not even feel satisfaction. Instead, as she watched the events unfolding before her, she felt hollowed out—and a deep sense of regret. Now that her plans had become a reality, she could not help but admit that there was a part of her that still loved her people, that still wanted to be loved and accepted by them. That wanted them alive, that wanted things to be the way they used to be.

She had thought all this destruction would make her so happy. But now that there was nothing left, for some reason, she felt sad. She did not know why. Perhaps it was because with her people and land destroyed, there was nothing left to remember her time on earth. Nothing left that was familiar in the world. All that remained now was Romulus and his Empire—all these awful creatures.

As Luanda looked at Romulus's broad back rippling with muscles, a commander at the height of his powers, ready to conquer every last inch of the world, a tremendous hatred for him built up inside her. He was to blame for all of this. She hated the way he treated her. Like a piece of property. She hated how subservient she had been forced to become to him. She despised everything about him.

Romulus's soldiers were all preoccupied on deck, and Romulus stood alone at the bow of the boat, his back to all, Luanda the only one allowed to get close to him, hardly ten feet away. She glanced around one last time to make sure no one was looking, then, secretly she tightened her grip on the hilt of the dagger she kept hidden in her belt. She squeezed so hard, she could feel her knuckles turning white. She imagined herself strangling Romulus as she squeezed.

Luanda took a step forward, towards Romulus's exposed back, a cold gust of wind and ocean spray striking her in the face.

Then another step.

Then another.

Luanda could not rectify wrongs, could not change what she had already done, the mistakes she had already made. She could not bring her homeland back. She could not restore the Shield.

But there was still one thing she could do, time for one last remaining act of redemption before she died. She could kill a barbarian. She could murder Romulus. She would get vengeance, at least, for herself, and vengeance, at least, for all of them. If she could not have anything else in life, at least she could have that.

Luanda tightened her grip as she extracted the dagger and took another step. She was but two steps away, seconds away from killing this monster. She knew that she herself would be captured and killed shortly thereafter—but she no longer cared—as long as she succeeded.

There he stood, so smug, so arrogant. He had underestimated her—like all of them. He had seen her as property, as someone not to be feared. Luanda had been underestimated her entire life. Now she was determined to make him—and every other man in her life—pay. With one stroke of the blade, her life would find satisfaction.

Luanda took the last step, raised her dagger high, and anticipated the satisfying feeling of her blade puncturing his flesh and putting an end to this creature's life for good. She could already see it happening, could see him dropping to his knees, collapsing face first, dead.

Luanda plunged the blade down with all her might—and yet, the strangest thing happened. The blade suddenly stopped as the tip hit his back. It was like hitting steel—it could not puncture the skin. It hovered there in midair, and no matter how hard she tried to push it down, it just would not enter his skin. It was as if he were protected by a magic shield.

Romulus turned around, slowly, calmly, a smile on his face as he shook his head and stared back at her, holding the blade in midair, harmlessly. Luanda looked at the blade, wondering what had happened.

Romulus shook his head.

"It was a good attempt," he said. "And any other time, you would have killed me. But you see," he said, leaning in close, his pungent breath in her face, "while this moon lasts, I am invincible. To every man, to every blade, to everything of this earth. Including you and your dagger."

Romulus leaned back and laughed, then reached out and calmly took the blade from her hand. She was helpless to stop him. He raised it high, grimaced, then suddenly stepped forward and plunged it into her heart.

Luanda gasped as she felt the cold metal entering her heart. She felt her heart stop, felt all the life and air leaving her body, felt her body go limp, numb, felt herself collapse to the wooden deck of the ship. She looked up and saw Romulus's laughing face before her eyes closed for the last time, realizing that nothing in the world would stop Romulus. Nothing.

Her final thoughts, before all life left her, were, strangely enough, of her father.

*Father,* she thought, *I never meant to disappoint you. Forgive me.*

# CHAPTER THIRTY-ONE

Thorgrin fell through the air, yelling, flailing, feeling the cold air rush past him at breathtaking speed as he plummeted for the ocean and the cliffs below. He fell hundreds of feet, feeling his entire life rush by. He knew that in moments he would land, dead, and it would all be over, here, on these rocks, at this ocean, so close to finding his mother. Here, in this Land of Druids, land of dreams. He wondered how it could be, how it was possible that he could strive for something his entire life only to have it slip away, just out of his grasp.

Somehow, he had failed. He had become the greatest warrior he could be on the battlefield; and yet, he had not conquered the depths of his own psyche. The one opponent left in the world whom he could not defeat was himself.

He'd been defeated by himself. What did that mean? He tried to understand it, at lightning speed, as he fell. To him, it meant that there must be some part of himself that was stronger than another part. A part that could defeat himself. A part that was so strong, it could overcome anything. It was a great force within him.

Thor had a sudden realization: that great force, even it was destructive, was still a part of him. It was still a force that could be harnessed. Which meant that he could find that dark part of himself, and harness it for the good. Energy was energy—it just needed to be redirected. Perhaps he could get that part of himself to work for him, instead of against him. If Thor could use that power to defeat himself, perhaps he could tap it to save himself.

Thor closed his eyes as he fell through the air, and he tried to summon his inner power, the power of his mind. He had been relying too much on his physical side his entire life, he realized. He was starting to realize that his mind was just as powerful as his body—if not more so. He could use his mind to do wonderful, miraculous things, things that his body could not.

Thorgrin focused, and as he did, he used the power of his mind to slow the world, to slow the very fabric in the air.

Thorgrin felt the world slow, then come to a stop. He felt himself floating in midair, frozen in the fabric of time and space. He felt the part of himself that was creating the time and space. He felt the infinite power within himself, the power that was not separate from the universe. He tapped into the endless stream of energy flowing through the universe, as Argon had often taught him, and he felt himself right in the center of it.

Thor held his hands out wide, palms up, and felt his fingertips and palms tingling through the very fabric of the sky. They felt as if they were on fire, burning with energy.

Thor went deeper, until he reached the place in his mind where he began to see no separation between his mind and the universe, between the energy flowing into him from the universe, and the energy flowing out. He began to see that he could control it. He could control his environment. He could also create everything around him. He saw that he could create his circumstance. And that his mind and his energy were more powerful than the manifestation he was in.

Thor commanded himself, the part of himself he could not control, the darkest part of himself. He commanded it to stop manifesting this circumstance. To change everything around him. And in the process, he forced himself to stop resisting, to let the universe be what it was. To let himself be who he was. Once he felt a complete acceptance of the universe, a complete acceptance of himself, then a deep peace overcame him, a peace unlike he had ever felt.

Thor slowly opened his eyes, and he knew, before he saw anything, that the universe around him had changed. He'd stopped himself from falling, and instead, was now floating upwards, gently, higher and higher, turning to an upright position, faster and faster, until he reached the top of the cliff. He set himself down gently, and he stood before his mother's castle.

There was no longer any danger, no longer any fear. He'd gone to his deepest depths, and he'd risen above it. Here he was, alone, facing the entrance to his mother's castle. He'd crossed the skywalk, the

201

place he could never cross in his dreams. He had finally managed to cross to the other side.

Thor examined the castle in awe. Before him were two huge, golden arched doors, five times as tall as he, and five times as wide. They shone so brightly they nearly blinded him, each with massive handles carved in the shape of a falcon.

Thor sensed intuitively that grasping those handles and trying to open the door would do no good. He knew it was a magic door, the most powerful door in the world. That the only way in was if the doors were opened for him.

Thor waited for them to open, but they did not.

"I demand to be let in!" Thor boomed out.

"You are not worthy of being let in here," boomed out a voice, dark, male.

Thor stood his ground, determined.

"I am worthy!" Thor yelled back, feeling worthy for the first time.

"And why are you worthy?" came the voice.

"I am Thorgrin. Son of my mother, Queen of the Land of the Druids. Son of Andronicus, King of the Empire. I am he. I, and no other. I am not worthy because of my powers. I am not worthy because of my skills. I am worthy because of *who I am*. I *deserve* to be let inside these doors. For no other reason than for *who I am*."

Thor felt his entire body vibrating as he spoke the words. He felt that he had finally reached the deepest truth of this training. Acceptance of himself.

He began to see that everything he manifested in the universe was a result of how he felt about himself. All the dark forces, they were real, and yet they were also all figments of himself he had to overcome. The deepest, hardest foe to overcome was how he felt about himself.

He had viewed himself his entire life, he realized it now, as undeserving. He still did now. When he let go of that, when he accepted himself fully and completely, just for who he was, then all doors in the universe would open for him. That was the final step towards conquering himself.

202

Thor felt a deep sense of peace as he realized all of this, as he accepted himself.

He opened his eyes slowly, and he looked up to see the doors shining more brightly than they ever had, and opening, slowly, wider and wider, the most beautiful sound in the world as the hinges opened effortlessly. Light flooded him, a golden light, pouring out from inside the castle, all-embracing, warmer, stronger than he could imagine.

He took his first step. Then another.

He felt warmer and warmer, and he knew that in just a few more steps, he would be inside this castle, with his mother. Finally, his destiny would be complete. In just a few more steps, all would be revealed.

And his life would never be the same again.

## CHAPTER THIRTY-TWO

Alistair found herself flying, looking down over the Ring, and she did not know how. She had no wings, she rode on no dragon, and yet still she floated, soaring above the landscape of her home country, looking down at it all from above.

As she looked down, she was confused. In place of the summer bounty she had left, in place of the fertile fields, the endless orchards she had grown accustomed to, there was a scorched land beneath her, destroyed by the dragons' breath. Nothing was left—not a single city, town, village, not even a hamlet. Every last structure had been burned to ashes.

The trees, once so lush, ancient, were all burnt-out stumps, and there were no more structures to mark the landscape. There remained nothing but waste and devastation.

Alistair was horrified. She flew low, covering the entire Ring, and found herself flying over the Canyon, over the great crossing. She saw below her Romulus, leading an army of millions, stretching as far as the eye could see. The Empire now occupied her homeland.

Alistair knew then that her homeland had been destroyed forever, and the Shield destroyed with it. The Ring was occupied, was now the property of the Empire. What once was would never be again.

Alistair blinked and found herself standing before her mother's castle, her back to it, facing a great skywalk, which twisted and turned its way miles below to the mainland. It was a long, curving path, and on it there walked a sole figure. He came close, and she realized it was her brother, Thorgrin, here to see their mother.

Thor looked up at Alistair, and she was so relieved to see her brother, the last person alive in a world of desolation. She felt that in moments she'd be meeting their mother, the three of them together for the first time.

Thor came close and smiled as he held out a hand for her. She reached for him.

Suddenly, the skywalk beneath him collapsed, and Thor fell through it, plummeting through the air and toward the rocks and ocean below.

Alistair looked down and watched, helpless, her heart breaking; without thinking, she dove down, over the cliff, to save him.

"Thorgrin!" she cried.

Alistair found herself landing not in the ocean but rather on an entirely new landscape, atop a plateau, looking down over thousands of people of the Southern Isles. She turned and saw Erec standing beside her, holding her hand, each of them dressed in their wedding attire, in luxurious silk robes.

But something was wrong with Erec when he smiled: he smiled wider, and blood poured from his mouth. He then collapsed, falling face first off the edge of the cliff, arms out wide by his side, trailing blood, as his people reached out to grab him with open arms. Alistair lifted her hands, covered in blood, and found herself standing there alone, her groom diving, dead, into the masses below.

"Erec!" she screamed.

Alistair woke screaming, breathing hard, looking all around her in the predawn light of her chamber. She wiped sweat from her brow and jumped from her bed, searching her hands for blood.

But there was none.

Alistair, confused, tried to catch her breath as she paced the room, rubbing her face, trying to understand where she was. It took her several moments to realize it had all been a dream. She was safe. Erec was safe. Thorgrin was safe. She was not in the Ring but here, safe, in the Southern Isles.

Alistair breathed. It was the most horrible dream she'd ever had. It felt like more than a dream—it felt like a message. Like a twisted version of the future. And it looked very dark.

Alistair tried to shake it off, pacing in her chamber. What could be the meaning of such a dream? She tried to assure herself that it was just night panic—yet deep down, in her gut, she could not help but feel that it was something more. Was her homeland really destroyed? Was her brother about to die?

Her groom?

Surely, such travesty couldn't all befall her at once; surely, it all meant nothing.

Alistair crossed the room and splashed cold water on her face several times. She went to the open window, soft ocean breezes rolling in, and examined the Southern Isles in the predawn light. It was still the most beautiful view she had ever seen, the smell of orange blossoms waking her, the moist air calming her. It was the cleanest she'd ever breathed.

Alistair looked out at the perfect landscape, saw all the people already up, already preparing for the big wedding that day, and felt certain that in a place like this, surely no evil could befall them.

Alistair sighed, shook her head, and chided herself. Just fancies in the night, she told herself. Just fancies in the night.

*

The first morning sun rose in the sky, and Alistair sat in her bridal chamber, surrounded by a dozen attendants giggling and laughing, all of them elated as they helped her prepare. As one of them made a final adjustment on her dress, Alistair stepped forward as others pulled up a huge polished glass. She stood there, heart pounding in excitement, and saw her reflection.

Alistair gasped; she had never looked so striking. She wore the most beautiful dress she'd ever seen, all white, made of lace, covering her from her neck to toe, and a veil to match the long white gloves. She had never considered herself to be pretty, despite how the men in her life had reacted to her, yet now, looking at herself like this, she felt she wasn't as ugly as she had thought.

"It is the dress I wore at my wedding," Erec's mother said, smiling, coming up beside her, laying a gentle hand on her shoulder. "On you it's even more beautiful. That is how it was meant to be worn."

206

Erec's mother embraced her, and Alistair had never felt so filled with joy. She could not wait for the ceremony.

Erec's mother led her to the door, and she opened it, and pointed to a copper walkway.

"The path leads you to your groom's chamber," she said. "Go to him. He awaits you. He shall lead you to the ceremony."

Alistair turned to her, touched.

"I don't know how to thank you," she said, more grateful than she could express.

Erec's mother embraced her.

"I shall be lucky to have a daughter like you."

Alistair turned onto the copper walkway alone, making her way on the short walk toward a beautiful, small marble house, open-aired, columns on all sides, in which she knew Erec awaited her.

As she reached its entrance, she looked inside and saw Erec looking more regal than she had ever seen him, dressed in light chainmail, covered by a silk white mantle, a gold crown on his head. He paced nervously, clearly waiting for her, and she was sure he was excited, given how much longer it had taken her to get ready.

She thought of rushing to him, but then she decided she wanted to surprise him; she wanted to see the look on his face when she walked in the door.

"My lord!" she called out playfully, hiding behind a column. "Close your eyes and count to five! I want to surprise you!"

He laughed.

"For you, anything," he said. "I cannot count fast enough!"

She could hear the excitement in his voice, like a little boy.

"Slowly, my love!" she called back.

"One," he called out, slowly. "Two...Three..."

Alistair made a final adjustment to her veil, then began to walk into the room.

"Four!" he called out.

She entered and looked at him, his eyes closed, beaming—and suddenly, her smile dropped. She saw something she could not understand. It was like something out of a nightmare: racing into the room, from the rear side of the open-air chamber, was a sole figure, sprinting at full speed, a sword in hand. An assassin.

He sprinted right for Erec's back—but Erec stood there, smiling, eyes closed, unsuspecting as he awaited her.

It was happening so fast, and Alistair was so shocked, so unprepared for the sight, she could barely summon the words to warn him. They caught in her throat as it went dry.

"Erec!" she finally managed to shout, panicked, just as the man reached him.

Erec suddenly opened his eyes and looked at her, concern in his face.

By then, it was too late. The figure—whom Alistair now recognized as Bowyer, the Alzac warrior Erec had defeated in the contest—had already reached Erec. He raised his sword behind him, and with a guttural cry, he lowered it—stabbing Erec in the back.

Erec cried out, and Alistair cried out louder. He dropped to his knees, blood gushing from his mouth, from his back. Bowyer left the sword in Erec's back as he turned and sprinted away as fast as he had entered.

"My love!" Erec cried, reaching a hand out for Alistair as he collapsed.

"NO!" Alistair shrieked, losing all sense of herself, as if she were watching someone else's nightmare unfolding before her.

Alistair ran to Erec's side and collapsed beside him, cradling him, his blood pouring all over her dress.

"Alistair, my love," he said weakly.

She felt him dying her arms, felt his life slipping away as she wept, gut-wrenching cries that filled the room, radiated beyond, rose to heaven. She knew it was too late. And she felt that it was all her fault—she had distracted him with her stupid game. Erec surely would have seen the man coming otherwise if he had not closed his eyes and waited for her. She had inadvertently helped kill the man that she would die for. The man she loved more than anything in the world would soon.

Her wedding day had arrived—and the love of her life was dead.

# CHAPTER THIRTY-THREE

Gwendolyn stood on the upper ramparts of Tirus's fort, looking out at the horizon, as she had been for hours, watching the sea. Her expression was grim as she held Guwayne in her arms, Argon's words thundering in her mind. Had everything Argon said been right? Or had they just been the words of a dying, delusional man?

Gwen wanted to think the latter, but she could not help but fear his words were true.

As she looked out, as she watched and waited, the cold wind brushing her face, she had a sinking feeling that her time here on earth had come to an end. She felt an inevitability to her life now, as if they had come to their final resting place here on these craggy, desolate isles. She wished, more than anything, that Thorgrin were here, that he would return and be by her side. With him by her side, she felt as if she could face anything.

Yet somehow she knew that he would not. She prayed for his safety. She prayed that, wherever he was, he would be okay. That he would remember her. Remember Guwayne.

As Gwen blinked, watching the clouds, suddenly, on the most distant horizon, something came into view. At first it was very faint: it was a motion, a movement in the dark clouds. Then she saw wings, one set, then another. A dragon came into view. Then another.

Then another.

Gwen's heart sank as her worst nightmares came to life: a host of dragons filled the distant horizon, screeching angrily, flapping their great wings. It was death, she knew, coming for them all.

"Sound the bells," Gwendolyn said calmly to Steffen, who stood waiting patiently nearby.

Steffen turned and ran off, and up and down the ramparts bells tolled, warning her people. Down below shouts arose, as people scrambled to take cover, running into caves, to underground passages, as Gwen had prepared them—anywhere they could to escape the dragons' breath.

Deep down, Gwen knew it was a futile effort. Nothing could escape a dragon's wrath—much less the wrath of a host of dragons. She knew that whomever the dragons missed, Romulus's men would finish off.

Moments later, Gwendolyn saw the ocean fill with black. There were black ships—Empire ships—as far the eye could see. It was an entire world of ships; she did not know so many ships could exist in the world. She marveled that all of them would want to descend on such a small island. That all of them were coming just for her.

Gwen suddenly heard a screech overhead, so close, and she looked up, wondering, bracing herself. She was shocked to see Ralibar. He had appeared from somewhere on the island, screeching, flapping his great wings, his talons extended. She assumed that he would be flying away, away from the destruction that came for them, that he would save himself.

But to her surprise, Romulus flew straight ahead, flying out, all alone, to greet the oncoming army. He flew with all his might, and he did not slow as he sped to bravely face them all. Gwen's heart soared at Ralibar's courage. He knew he would die facing them, and yet he did not flinch in battle. This one dragon, so bold, so proud, flying up to sacrifice his life, to die in battle, to defend Gwendolyn and all her people—and to take out as many dragons as he could.

Gwendolyn clutched Guwayne tighter, turned from the ramparts, and hurried down the spiral stone stairs. The time had come.

*

Gwendolyn walked quickly and deliberately along the rocky shoreline by the ocean's edge, clutching Guwayne, the two of them all alone. Far off, she could hear the dragons cry, and she knew it was too close; there wasn't much time left now.

Gwen listened to the sound of the waves lapping gently on the shore of this smooth bay on the rear of the island that led out to the

210

ocean, its current strong as the tide was pulling out to sea. She walked over to a small boat, one which she'd had made just for this purpose, eight feet long, with a mast just as high and a small sail. The boat was large enough for a child.

A single child.

Gwen sobbed as she clutched Guwayne tight one last time, leaned over, and kissed him. She kissed him for as long as she could, until Guwayne began to cry.

As Gwen began to lower him, he grabbed her hair and pulled it. She continued to lower him until he was safely in his bassinet inside the boat, wrapped up in blankets and wearing his wool hat.

Gwendolyn sobbed, kneeling by his side, as Guwayne wailed.

Gwen looked out at the ocean, at the horizon, and her heart was torn in two. She could not bear the thought of sending her child out there into the unknown. Yet she knew it would be selfish to keep him here with her. Staying here meant an instant and cruel death. Out there, he would probably die, too. But at least he might have a chance. It might be one chance in a million, floating somewhere, out there, on the vast and open sea. But who knew where the tides, where the fates, might take him. Perhaps, she prayed, they would take him to safety. To a mother and father who loved him. Perhaps he could be raised by someone else, become a great warrior, live the life he was meant to live. Maybe, just maybe, this child would have a chance, could live on for them. She wished, more than anything, that she could give this to him; but she knew she could not.

"I love you, my child," she said, meaning every word, unable to hold back her tears.

And with those final words, she knelt down, grabbed the boat, and gave it a shove.

It was a small boat, and it rocked as she shoved it into the calm waters. The light current slowly and gently pulled it out to sea. Guwayne's cries, instead of fading, grew louder and louder as the current pulled him, all alone, into the expanse of an empty, gray sea.

211

Gwendolyn watched him go, his eyes flashing, the color of the sea, and she could not take the sight anymore; she closed her eyes and prayed her last prayer with all that she had:

*Please, God. Be with him.*

**COMING SOON!**

**BOOK #12 IN THE SORCERER'S RING**

Please visit Morgan's site, where you can join the mailing list, receive a free book, listen to audio, receive a free APP, hear exclusive news, see additional images, and find links to stay in touch with Morgan on Facebook, Twitter, Goodreads and elsewhere!

www.morganricebooks.com

**Books by Morgan Rice**

# THE SORCERER'S RING
## A QUEST OF HEROES
## A MARCH OF KINGS
## A FEAST OF DRAGONS
## A CLASH OF HONOR
## A VOW OF GLORY
## A CHARGE OF VALOR
## A RITE OF SWORDS
## A GRANT OF ARMS
## A SKY OF SPELLS

# THE SURVIVAL TRILOGY
## ARENA ONE (BOOK #1)
## ARENA TWO (BOOK #2)

# the Vampire Journals
## turned (book #1)
## loved (book #2)
## betrayed (book #3)
## destined (book #4)
## desired (book #5)
## betrothed (book #6)
## vowed (book #7)
## found (book #8)
## resurrected (book #9)
## craved (book #10)